THE HIGHGATE MURDER

S J ANDREWS

Copyright © 2021 by S J Andrews

All rights reserved.

No part of this book may be reproduced in any form or by any electronic or mechanical means, including information storage and retrieval systems, without written permission from the author, except for the use of brief quotations in a book review.

This book is a work of fiction and there is no intended resemblance to persons living or dead.

A word on spelling

UK spelling has been used within this book.

For Michael

1

In the immortal words of Kinsey Millhone: I killed a man and it's weighing heavily on my mind.

Other things I have in common with the legendary lady: I'm in my thirties, I'm a PI and I'm alone.

My eyes scan my shelves of crime fiction, books double stacked and piled high, Golden Age to the hard-boiled seventies, Athens-under-the-junta Costas Haritos to original Scandi-crime copper Martin Beck. Some of those beaten-up paperbacks I've had since I was a kid.

These walls of books aren't in the office. They'd surely set a few alarm bells ringing if clients came in here to see my primary motivation for doing this job was a lifetime of getting a kick out of mysteries.

Despite life's knocks, I've always been able to sit in a chair, crack open a mystery and lose myself for a while. In this draughty Highgate flat, I read, my pap's old jazz records playing in the background. It helped deal with the chaos of this existence. I had the flat, the music, my books, my work, and that was working for me.

Until now.

There's a big difference between the convenient victim killed with a candlestick in the library, and a real-life corpse, especially if the blood is on your hands.

I was staring at my hands when a knocking at the door disturbed the silence.

It started a week ago, when Edward Donsaw came to my office. He'd made the three o'clock appointment by phone the day before.

At twenty minutes past the hour, there was no sign of him, and I was mindlessly looking out the window. I live in a run of Victorian terraced houses on the Archway Road, all three storeys high, ornate and crowned with Dutch gables. Once red-bricked and elegant, now near-black from years of London smog.

At the base of these buildings are a run of no-nonsense businesses: barbers, estate agents, greasy-spoon cafes catering bacon and eggs for the lorry drivers on their long-distance journeys into the city.

A house sliced into three low-ceiling flats, my office-apartment sits between an old boozer who lives and sells used furniture on the ground floor, and a kid in her twenties upstairs, who makes a living online gambling (so she tells me). I'm stuck in the middle in more ways than one. I'm too old for Emma Westmore, upstairs, to take any interest in me, yet I'm not like Joel Brown, down below, grey-haired, strawberry-nosed, a man who spends most of his time standing in the pub over the road, forever tending to a pint of London Pride.

The office contains a desk, four chairs, and file boxes on shelves — containing bills, receipts and other bits of life admin, but it makes the room look more like a place of business.

The Archway Road is a miserable main road, and part of the Great North Road that goes all the way up to Scotland. In days of yore, people would stop here for the night at a coaching inn to avoid getting murdered by highwaymen, and that's how this old north London village originated.

Out the window and across the traffic of the Archway Road is a fine view of Highgate Wood, and beyond that, Queen's Wood, both part of an ancient woodland; miles of nature where locals walk their dogs in the mostly cool, misty weather.

I saw a red MG, its finish sprinkled with rust, park in front of my building. A man I presumed to be Donsaw got out of the car and pressed the buzzer for my office. I buzzed him in and opened my door. The light in my flat provided the illumination he needed to get up the stairs. The hallway light hadn't worked for some time.

He looked like an elderly playboy, dashing, with thick white hair, dressed in a white shirt, open at the neck, and shabby chinos like a millionaire who didn't care. He'd once had fingernails but they'd been bitten away. He was a little taller than me, which put him at about 6'2.

He shook my hand and followed me through the narrow hallway to my office. He looked around, saw there was nothing much to look at, and took a seat on the other side of the desk, crossing his long legs. I asked what I could do for him.

'It's a delicate matter,' Donsaw said in aristocratic tones. He'd also said this yesterday, on the phone. Today, he elaborated. 'There's a young man. He's in trouble. I have a connection to the family, knew his mother.'

I nodded.

'Mr Seferis, do you know about the fire in Highgate village?'

I shrugged and shook my head. Highgate village was a short walk up the hill from my place, but I hadn't noticed any burning buildings lately.

'The fire was in his place of residence, Pond Square Mansions, the block of flats behind the high street.'

'When was this?'

'A few days ago now.' He took an elaborate deep breath and paused for effect. 'Mr Seferis, they're blaming Neddy for the fire.'

'*Neddy?*'

Donsaw rolled his eyes conspiratorially, his charm easy and practised. 'His mother named him, *Neddy Mara*. The fire department arrived, put the fire out and inspected the damage and causation. They judged it was a case of careless outdoor cooking and put it down to negligence.

'The other tenants in the building had other plans. They have such a dislike for him, they started kicking up a fuss, insisting he did it on purpose. It's likely they're trying to get out of having their insurance cover the damages. They got together and conspired, then went to the police, saying he'd threatened them, that they'd witnessed him taking drugs. Because of their testimony, the police are now working on the angle that Neddy is an arsonist.'

'That's some serious dislike,' I said.

'It *is* serious,' Donsaw agreed. 'It would mean prison time and a criminal record. He had one of his gatherings that evening, so it stands to reason this was a light-hearted social that led to an accident, not a vindictive plot to do anyone any harm. Nobody saw him starting this fire.'

'If that's the case, I don't think the testimony of these

angry neighbours would be enough to convict him,' I said. 'All you need is a good lawyer to present the facts.'

'I've *hired a* good lawyer.'

'The police can do the rest,' I said.

Donsaw dismissed the suggestion with a wave of the hand. 'I want someone who works for *me.*'

I supposed people like him usually did.

'I want to feel like I've done all that I can,' he said. 'I want the best. I heard about what happened with your wife.'

I focused my efforts on not breaking eye contact. 'What does Neddy say happened?'

Donsaw looked into space. He suddenly looked a lot older, perhaps a method for avoiding questions he didn't want to answer.

I tried another question. 'Why would his neighbours have such a dislike for him?'

'Neddy is a famous music performer,' Donsaw answered, no small amount of pride in his voice. 'He has a run of pretty women chasing him. That's a cause for jealousy.'

'Fame can be a dangerous game,' I said.

'Indeed.'

'Does he sing? Play an instrument?'

Donsaw shrugged. 'I'm too old for all that,' he said, and gestured at his ears. 'My hearing's practically gone.'

When it suits you, I thought. I asked him, 'Would I communicate with your lawyer directly?'

'No,' he said.

Laconic.

'Okay.' I leaned forward. 'Mr Donsaw, did Neddy tell you he wasn't responsible for the fire?'

Donsaw's gaze became vague again, but I waited him out. 'He didn't, as such. We don't really speak.'

'You don't speak?'

'There's bad blood in the family, Mr Seferis.'

I nodded. I waited.

'I'm behind the scenes,' he said. 'Trying to fix things with the resources I have.'

I didn't have to take the case. I had my expenses covered for a period, and other cases would come along before too long. But something wasn't adding up. He was telling me only what he wanted me to know. My interest was piqued.

'Do you have Neddy's contact details?'

'I don't. We haven't spoken in a long time.'

'Bad blood.'

'Exactly.' He made a show of inspecting the remains of his fingernails. 'Do *you* have family, Mr Seferis?'

'I don't.'

'I suppose, as a result of what happened to you, you know a bit about Lady Fame yourself?'

I looked at him blankly. He wasn't the only one who could play that game.

'You must have been a good policeman.'

I shrugged.

'Why did you leave the job?'

I sighed and thought up an answer. 'I wanted to be a detective on my own terms. I don't have a boss to answer to. I choose my clients as and when I please. How did you learn about the fire?'

'It was big news,' he said. 'It happened in the heart of historical Highgate village. I read *Ham and High*.'

That was the neighbourhood's local paper. I saw it on all the news-stands, but I'd never looked inside it. The 'Ham' stood for Hampstead, Highgate's neighbouring village, that bit prettier and starting to be infiltrated by tourist routes.

'And what do *you* do from day-to-day?' I asked. This was

a phrasing I used on people who seemed like they'd retired, to bypass hearing the closed, obvious answer.

'Back in the day, I dabbled in a few things, politics, music. I used to arrange tennis tournaments featuring famous players. I've campaigned to save the parts of the village from developers...' He trailed off.

I paused to coax something more out of him. He finally said, 'Money isn't an issue. Can I write you a cheque?'

We hadn't discussed fees yet. I said he could. He brought a cheque book out of his inside blazer pocket, took a biro lying on the desk and wrote a ten-thousand-pound cheque. I wondered if he'd made a mistake with his zeroes.

'Mr Donsaw, this is *much* more than I charge for looking into something like this.'

Donsaw waved the protest away. 'I like dealing in round numbers. If you get results, it will be more than worth it. If you don't, it makes up for my wasting your valuable time.'

I said, 'My time isn't so valuable.'

2

Donsaw left. I opened my laptop and got online. I thought Neddy Mara would be an easy name to get a handle on, but there was no sign of him. Old man Donsaw knew him so little, I had to wonder if he actually existed.

I typed *music* beside his name.

Nothing.

I found the fire department's report. There *had* been a fire at Pond Square Mansions, but that didn't mention him either. The report was brief, only saying the fire on the roof of the building required four fire engines. The cause was as yet unknown. No casualties. No mention of any names, blame or celebrity.

So, doubtful Donsaw would have discovered Neddy's involvement through the press. But there was a community in this village-like neighbourhood and word got around. Highgate isn't London proper, where you can enjoy complete anonymity, but it's not a countryside village where everyone knows each other's business. It's the low-ceiling flat somewhere in-between. This wasn't something Donsaw would have needed a detective to find out. But I had to wonder how close an eye he kept on this young man who apparently had no idea a fairy godfather was looking out for him.

Ironically, with everything he'd said about fame, the man who'd just been in my humble home-office was easy to find online. He was nobility, a viscount.

I had to look up the meaning of viscount. It was a hereditary title that put him below an earl and above a baron. I wondered what the earl and baron would have to say about that.

I found a website that belonged to a local tour guide. It featured pictorial highlights of north London and he'd posted a picture of Donsaw's house, one of those big houses on the Highgate side of Hampstead Heath.

This was looking to be the most conveniently local case I'd ever worked. A fifteen-minute southerly walk from my place is Highgate village. Keep walking in that direction for another ten minutes, and you came to Donsaw's residence. That put Donsaw and Neddy in intriguing proximity for two people who never communicated.

A little research and I discovered his sons were Robert and William Donsaw. Robert had done nothing worthy of being featured on the world wide web, or nothing that *I* could find, at least. But William had a profile on the London Classical Piano Festival website, mentioning that he was the co-founder of the festival and his father's son. A dated, colour photograph showed a smiling, chubby, clean-shaven face, crowned with a messy mop of brown hair.

I had no contact details to work with and a leisurely walk to the nearby location appealed to me. I walked the fifteen minutes up the hill to Highgate village. The community fought valiantly to resist development, making it a cosy haven almost lost in time — but for the busy main road of endless traffic that cut through the antique high street.

Hidden behind the set of buildings that made up the west side on the high street was Pond Square. It took its name from a historical pond that had to be filled out when locals were using it for too many purposes: bathing, cleaning clothes, and eventually making themselves ill when using it as a source of drinking water.

A few benches and tall plane trees, gnarly and beautiful, created dappled shade on the gravelled area. Surrounding it were some of the oldest houses in London, some dating from the seventeenth century, and some of them very quaint in their odd, inconvenient shape and size. One that stood out for me had the dimensions of a two-storey car unit.

Taking up the north-west corner was a vast Gothic house, probably once owned by a well-to-do nobleman, and since converted into a jigsaw of luxury apartments. I could see the fire damage. The top roof had black patches and holes showing the building's wooden frame.

There were five buttons on the intercom. I pressed the highest number, which had the name 'Lindgren' beside it. After a few seconds, a male voice answered.

'Detective Seferis here about the roof. I'm waiting for an assistant. Will you be here in an hour?'

'Oh, um, yes.' The voice was young and polite.

I thanked the voice and said I'd be back shortly, then I walked away from the house, not wanting to be in earshot of any residents, to call Bill, a SOCO — scenes of crime officer — and old buddy from the Met. 'Alright, mate,' he said in his relaxed way. I explained the case to him and offered him an (unofficial) hundred-quid fee for his help, and a taxi here and back home for his trouble.

He said he might be able to find some time later in the

week. I told him I'd also get him a pint in a nearby pub with a nice beer garden. He said he'd be with me straight after work. I made a mental note to offer alcoholic refreshment first next time.

It was another cold summer's day in London town, and I headed straight for the shelter of The Gatehouse on the high street. I nursed a pint while waiting for Bill. Booze makes me sleepy and morbid, but you can't sit in a pub and not order an alcoholic drink. Anyway, it was just the one.

The drink disappeared and I had another before heading out to meet Bill's taxi. Five-foot-seven, dark spiky hair, his forensic kit strapped across his shoulder, Bill got out of the car and we shook hands. He handed me a manila folder. I handed him an envelope with cash inside.

'Basic report is in there,' he said. 'Give me a call if you need any more specifics.' He'd skimmed the basics while he was extracting the report and confirmed what Donsaw had told me.

I took him back to the house. We got buzzed in and climbed five flights to the top flat. A handsome-faced young man with neat hair was waiting for us at the door. The door was still in its frame, but the frame had been axed through by firefighters to get to the fire.

Lindgren looked to be in his twenties, though he had one of those fresh faces that would stay boyish for a long time to come.

What I could see of his flat was just as neat and pretty. Framed art deco travel posters hung on the wall. *Visit Cuba. Visit California.* Everything was new and retro, a sixties-style radio with a walnut finish, a shiny record player connected to a speaker made to look like an old guitar amp.

'Do you want to come up?' he asked, indicating a portal in the ceiling that led to the roof terrace.

I took my notebook out of my jeans back pocket and said I wanted to confirm a few things. The boy I was talking to was Alex Lindgren. He was actually Swedish, which explained how his English was better than most English people's. He worked abroad a lot, doing something clever for a computer company.

He rented the apartment through a letting agency and had been there for a year. There was an unused second bedroom in the apartment. As he was hardly there, he realised he'd been bleeding money. So, a couple of weeks ago, he started subletting the second bedroom to one Neddy Mara, a musician, and a friend of a friend.

Alex had been away on business pretty much the entire time since Neddy had arrived. He'd been away on the night of the fire and had returned the following day to find his door frame unattached to the wall. He didn't seem too perturbed by either event.

'Is your flatmate around?'

'Neddy's gone,' Alex said. 'He didn't like the vibe in the house after what happened so he's renting somewhere else. He's paid up here for the three months of his lease agreement so I'm in no hurry to find another flatmate. It was generous of him.'

'Generous.' I nodded in agreement. 'Nice guy?'

'Sure.'

'Can you tell me anything more about what he was like?'

Alex shrugged. 'I don't know him that well. He's a musician, very focused on his music.'

'I haven't spoken to the neighbours yet, but it sounds like they really took offence to him.'

'Sure,' Alex said. 'I don't think they liked the loud music.'

'Yes, but, you know, the fire was originally put down as an accident. But they've kicked up such a fuss, it's now being investigated whether he started the fire with intent. Can you say why they'd feel that strongly? No threats exchanged? Or signs of drug abuse?'

'No,' Alex said with an easy, affable smile. He was a very laid-back character.

'Do you have his contact details?'

He did. I also took the landlord's details, though I didn't feel a necessity to speak to him for the time being.

Alex opened the roof window and pulled down a narrow ladder. Bill climbed through the hole to the remains of the roof terrace and I followed.

Emerging, I whistled at the panoramic view of London. St Paul's and all the new sky scrapers of the city glowed in a crisp summer light that had broken through the clouds.

The roof terrace was covered by a grey tarpaulin. Bill and I stripped it off to reveal the charred remains, and Bill began his methodical inspection.

I shadowed him for a while, then I tried the phone number for Neddy I got from Alex, only to get an automated message. I told Bill I was going to check on the neighbours and got a grunt in reply.

I WALKED down to the ground floor to work my way back up door-to-door. In the foyer was an incongruously cheap mailbox, a cardboard box with five drawers. The postman had chosen to dump all the letters on top of the box. By rifling through them, I was able to acquire the residents' full names and their location in the house.

It was early evening, late enough for the residents to be home from work. The stairwell held comforting cooking smells.

Gavin Morgan, a man of about forty with a guarded

expression, answered the door to Flat 1. I learned he was a homeowner who'd lived there for five years with his wife. They'd since had two kids, a three-year-old and a one-year-old. I asked what it was like having a party animal on the top floor.

'Too loud,' Morgan said. 'I messaged the landlord, hoping he'd do something about it. He only forwarded the message along to Neddy, which landed us right in it.'

I rolled my eyes. 'Nice of him.'

'Right?' Morgan said. 'As long as he's getting his four grand a month, he doesn't give a crap. Just doesn't want to be bothered.'

'What do you mean, *right in it*?'

'I mean, the kid was enough of an arsehole *before* he knew we contacted his landlord. After the text, I got a note in our mailbox, telling me to mind my own business and focus on looking after my family.'

'From Neddy?'

'Yes!'

I sighed and shook my head, expressing solidarity. 'Pretty basic mailbox, by the way.'

'Yeah,' Morgan said. 'We've been meaning to sort something better out, but we're a lazy bunch. Last time we got our act together to have a house meeting was over a year ago. Anyway,' he said, getting back to the matter at hand. 'Next time I pass him in the street, he follows up the note with a snarl and the question: *How's your family doing?*'

'The police have the note, right?' I asked.

'Yes,' Morgan said. 'He said something similar to everyone in the building. That's why we wanted him out of here. We didn't feel safe.'

Behind the door of Flat number 2 was Kate Strauss, a

young mother with a friendly smile and a Germanic accent. A cute toddler she called Rosie ran around behind her.

'Can't have been easy,' I said. 'Having Keith Richards upstairs.'

Kate answered in the sweetest, softest voice. 'Rosie's a deep sleeper.'

I wondered if she was a spiritual healer by profession. Or a florist.

'Must have been horrible, you and little Rosie standing outside on the night of the fire.'

Kate shrugged. There was no winding up some people. Her healer spirit was too strong. 'It happened on that really hot night, so it wasn't so bad.'

I remembered the evening well. I'd sat by an open window, next to a fan, with a cold beer, attempting to read a Rebus novel and not getting very far.

'So things are a bit more pleasant, now he's gone?'

Another shrug. 'Sure.'

'The tenants said they received threats from Neddy. Did you?'

Finally, her smile faded. 'We never spoke. But I told the police I did hear him shouting at the others. He'd really scream.'

'What did you hear?'

She sighed and lowered her voice so Rosie couldn't hear. '*Mind your own effing business*, and that kind of thing.' Her eyes lowered to the ground. She took a deep breath and looked back up at me. 'I told the police he also said he'd burn the house to the ground with all the arseholes in it. Now he's in trouble with the police. I just told the truth.'

'You have nothing to feel bad about then. You can't go wrong with the truth.'

Her eyes were lowered again.

'Rosie's a real cutie,' I said.

The smile reappeared. I left it at that.

THE BARTLETTS LIVED in Flat 3. The man of the house answered the door. He also downplayed his antipathy towards Neddy, out of a sense, it seemed, of being age-conscious. 'I hated to be that guy, knocking on the door and asking to turn the music down. I moved in seven years ago, early thirties. Now I'm forty. I used to get *invited* to the parties.' He laughed at the mysteries of ageing.

'But after having met Neddy, I guess it wasn't the party you'd like to be at anyway?'

Bartlett made a heavy sigh. 'Yeah, not the nicest of guys. First time I knocked — five in the morning, mind you, with me and the wife having work the next day — he said: *No can do. The DJ's busy snorting coke out of someone's arse crack.*'

'Classy.'

'That was the PG version. I'm sure every generation acts in a way the last generation scoffs at. My parents couldn't believe I wore ripped jeans.'

'What happened after the arse crack comment?'

'After that, if we ever knocked, he'd turn the music up, like he was making a game of it. I had to call the police on them eventually. I couldn't believe I had to be that guy.'

'What happened then?'

'It was hilarious. We heard it all. I guess they expected to slap his wrists and scare him. He shouted at them and told them where they could go. I thought he was going to get himself arrested. But they left. He scared them off!'

'Wow.'

'Yeah, we intercepted them as they were coming downstairs to ask what was happening. They said: *We're only community support officers. We're not here to enforce the law.* And they rushed off as quickly as they could.'

'And then?'

'Well, that very night, he was banging on our door, calling us names, saying he was going to *kill* us.'

'What did you do?'

'Just had to ignore him and wait it out. We were feeling sheepish after calling the police.'

'That's intimidating behaviour,' I coaxed.

Bartlett shrugged. 'Just a kid. Whenever I see myself being critical, I hear my dad's voice.' He made his voice deeper. '*Turn that bloody music down. You call that music?*'

MARTIN ASHI LIVED in the final flat. He looked to be in his forties and lived with his wife and son. I could hear them making clinking sounds in the kitchen behind him. It didn't take much coaxing to get him started. 'I've got nothing against Alex. He's a nice enough kid. Not very considerate. He let Neddy sublet, realised he didn't like the situation and ran off to go skiing for the entire time Sid Vicious was living up there.'

'Skiing? I thought he travelled for work?'

Martin rolled his eyes. 'Work? Always took his skiing gear.'

'He looks like a wealthy, well-travelled kid,' I said.

'He was definitely travelling well while his apartment was an all-night rave venue. I texted him on day one when Neddy was having his first all-nighter. He didn't even reply, just forwarded the message onto Neddy.'

'I'm sure that made things pleasant.'

Martin let out a hollow laugh.

'Did you get any threats?'

'Yeah.' Martin lowered his voice as his anger and intensity rose. 'Not. Very. Pleasant. I told it all to the police and I'd rather not repeat it.'

'Did he make a reference to starting a fire?'

'Yeah, second or third night, I banged on the ceiling. It was the middle of the night, I have a son here trying to sleep, school the next day. He shouts through the floor, *I'll burn the bloody place down, then you can have your peace and quiet.* That's the PG version.'

'Did you see him on the day of the fire?'

'No. That's something I'm thankful for. He and his mates had left to go clubbing when the fire was raging. I was awake because of what I thought were loud raindrops smattering on the roof. It was the fire crackling. It was after three in the morning. A passer-by saw it and started buzzing the door and screaming at us the house was on fire.'

'Lucky for you he was walking by.'

Martin closed his eyes, nodding solemnly. 'So lucky. They said if it'd blazed any longer, things could have ended up a lot differently.'

'Things getting back to normal now?'

Martin grimaced. 'Months of repair work ahead, and every flat has a leak. We had torrential rain for three solid days after the fire. I went up there to ask about putting a tarpaulin down over the fire damage, make it a little more water proof. They weren't having it. Neddy would only shout at us like an animal. When he was out and we spoke to Alex, he said he'd do something about it, but that was a lie; he just wanted to get back to his computer. The landlord wouldn't lift a finger.'

'There was no convincing Alex?'

'No, I wasn't going to push myself in. And I didn't want to be in there doing it myself, then have Neddy return and find me there. I don't know what the little psycho's capable of. We heard him screaming a lot through the floors. We worried some domestic abuse was going on, then we realised he was shouting at a dog.'

'Jesus.'

Martin's face was red with rage now as he relived it all. 'The things some people get away with,' he said. 'Water soaked into the foundations and was dripping from our ceiling.'

'But there's a tarpaulin there now,' I said.

Martin nodded. 'I kept badgering Simon, the landlord, until he told me — on day four after the fire — that the little bastard had gone so I could do as I please. Oh, thanks very much. So, I drove down to buy a tarpaulin, brought it up here. Alex, in his relaxed way, says: *Oh, I was going to do it myself but whatever.* And I get to put it down. This is after the three-day rainstorm. But it's down now.'

Martin shook his head like a man ready to put it all behind him. He repeated, 'It's done now.'

3

Back in Alex's flat, I asked him, 'I heard some nasty things about Neddy. How did he seem to you?'

'Seemed fine. I mean, I saw him so briefly.'

'You said he was a friend of a friend?'

'Our girlfriends are friends.'

I asked for and made a note of their names.

Bill *seemed* to be hard at work on the roof. He must have heard me coming. I cooled my heels, as far as I understand that phrase, and took in the view of London. Part of David Copperfield is set in Highgate, I read half of it when I moved here a year ago. Dickens described the view of London from here. 'A great vapour with lights twinkling through it.' Something like that. The same view, but two hundred or so years ago.

Bill interrupted my musings by exclaiming, 'Saboteur!' He turned to me with a dark, almost accusatory expression.

'What?'

'A person who commits or practises sabotage.'

'I'm aware of the literal meaning of the expression. I was querying the randomness of it.'

Bill took a slow intake of breath, composing himself — the boy was excited. 'Whoever told you there was more to this than meets the eye was onto something. Mike, someone did mean to start this fire.'

I crouched down next to him.

'Look at this,' he said, running his finger along a silver residue I could see in the crisp summer light, a light so perfect and a residue so faint, I doubted what I was looking at would be decipherable at any other moment.

'Traces of metallic sodium,' Bill said. 'If someone wanted a fire to eventually start somewhere, it can be stored in a container of oil. The container could be made so the elements slowly leak out, then when enough gets exposed to air or water, you have a small explosion, and — with all this wooden decking here with flammable tar beneath — a fire. And I'll tell you what else. If the container is made of wood, it would be the first thing to burn up, and there is no remaining evidence, except this faint trace of metallic sodium.'

'Are you sure?'

'As sure as David Caruso is a carrot top.'

'One hour before your first *CSI* reference.'

'Hey, it's a great show.'

'Yeah, anyway, how could this have been missed?'

'No one was looking for it. It's very subtle, very professional. No chance of fingerprints. You need a clean and shiny surface for that, despite what Caruso or one of his beautiful assistants would have you believe.'

'If the police are working on the assumption that Neddy started the fire, why wouldn't they *look* for it the way you just did?'

Bill shrugged. 'I've gone in looking for something to be wrong. They were going on the assumption that Neddy wanted to start a fire in his own flat after threatening everyone that he was going to do it. So why would he be surreptitious about it? Some oil and a match and you have the same result.'

'This is really going to land him in it, isn't it?' I said. 'I was supposed to help get him off the hook.'

'Hope you didn't start spending that paycheque of yours,' Bill said. 'Your client might want a refund.'

WE SAID GOODBYE TO ALEX, walked across Pond Square and saw The Gatehouse was too packed now to even get in the front door. We walked down the hill back towards my place. The Woodman is almost directly across the street from my flat, awkwardly positioned on a busy junction. It has a pleasant beer garden, sheltered from the main road by tall, leafy plane trees, but we were forced to drink inside by a cold drizzle.

There was an early Friday evening buzz within its wood-lined walls. Young friendship groups, with colourful hats and drinks, laughing and shouting; an older phase of drinkers — couples, two men, or a man and a woman, in more subdued clothing, with more subdued expressions, the men with a pint of beer, the women with a glass of wine; and then there were the old geezers, with their pints and crossword puzzles.

We leaned on the bar and I got us both a beer. I was already feeling the fatigue from the pair I'd had earlier, and wasn't in the mood for a drink, but you can't just buy a friend a beer and have a fizzy water for yourself, especially after they've just done you a favour. You don't *drink* a beer with someone, you *have a* beer, and that means having one yourself.

I was out of practice, slurring my words after the first round, and I didn't stop then. However adversely I felt its effects, with the consumption of a couple of drinks always comes the desire to consume a couple more. Our position, leaning on the bar, probably didn't help either.

'I was just thinking about you the other day,' Bill said. 'I'm going through all the Jean-Pierre Melville films, *Le Doulos, Le Cercle Rouge...*'

'That's how I like to be thought of,' I said. 'Do I remind you more of Belmondo or Alain Delon?'

'I wish. Just more the lone detective doing his thing, going after his man. You really are living the dream.'

'Some dream. Why all the French films? Are you educating Marion on the cinema of her own country?'

'Nah.' His eyes flickered to the floor for a second and he ran an awkward hand through his hair. 'We broke up.'

'Ah. Sorry to hear that, and you always wanted a French girlfriend.'

'Tell me about it. Finally, someone to watch the works of Godard and Truffaut with, but she just had too much of that feisty French temperament.'

'You prefer your drama on a screen.'

Bill rolled his eyes in agreement. 'Yes! Final straw was, my cousin stayed over one night. Marion came around unexpectedly and found us in bed together. She went ballistic.'

'You were in bed with your cousin?'

'Sure. I have a big bed. I wasn't going to make her sleep on the floor.'

'Were you wearing pyjamas or in your undies?'

'I can't believe you're taking her side.'

'I can understand it throwing her a little.'

'*A little* would be fair enough. But she refused to listen to any explanation, demanded we exchange our keys, not for the first time. She'd made us swap back and forth so often I didn't know whose set was whose. The tears and screaming, it was like living in an Alexandre Dumas novel.'

'That's tough,' I said.

'I hung in there as long as I could. She was from Le Havre. That's where Renoir filmed a lot of *La Bête Humaine*. We were talking about going together.'

'You were holding out for a trip with a local guide?'

Bill ran his hand through his hair again.

'Wow,' I said. 'Talk about objectification.'

'You're not thinking about dating at all?' Bill said, looking to change the subject. Then he winced at what he'd said and a silence ensued as we both struggled to come up with anything to say.

An almost welcome interruption appeared when someone sidled up to the bar behind me and said, 'Haven't seen you in The Woodman before.'

I turned to see a weathered face with full lips, a large gap between its front teeth, and no discernible eyebrows. Dark brown eyes stared at me in a deadpan expression.

An answer eluded me. It wasn't really a question. I shrugged, then thought to say, 'Here I am.'

A prolonged pause ended when Bill extended his hand. 'Bill Dun.' He jabbed his thumb at me. 'We're old colleagues.'

'Joel Brown,' said the owner of the weathered face. He shook Bill's hand. 'Mother was a fan of Joel McCrea.' It wasn't the first time I'd heard that introduction. It sounded like a reference to a bygone era, which was fitting, as he always wore a short-brimmed trilby that made him look a member of The Specials. I'd never seen his actual head in the decades I'd known him.

'Great taste,' Bill said. 'Sullivan's Travels is in my top hundred.'

'One of his best,' Joel said. 'I don't know why he settled into doing Westerns.'

'Ah, well, I read an interview where he said, as he got older, he felt better suited to them rather than playing an ageing leading man trying to look young, falling in love with pretty girls.'

'I can relate to that,' Joel said, looking at me for some input. When I didn't say anything, he told Bill, 'I live downstairs from this man. I get to hear him stomping around all evening. Just kidding.'

I nodded in acknowledgement of his humorous kid.

Without having ordered a drink, the barmaid appeared and presented him with a pint. He thanked her and took the drink in his big, chunky hand. He placed some change in her hand and closed her finger around it. 'Well, have a good night, boys.'

'You too,' Bill called out after him, then he said to me, 'Not a harmonious co-dwelling?'

'He gets nasty after a couple of drinks.'

'So you thought you'd get in there first with some pre-emptive iciness?'

'You don't want to get on my bad side,' I said. 'I can be as cold as a Mankell mystery.'

'So I see. What did he ever do?'

'It's a long story.'

Bill shrugged, like he didn't mind, or that he didn't mind if I minded.

'My old man was his landlord, had to deal with the complaints,' I said. 'Joel was a problem tenant. He used to live with his partner. He'd drink a lot, and shout and rave, until my dad had to drive down from Finchley to play peacemaker.'

'Why didn't he kick him out?'

I rolled my eyes. 'That wasn't his style. And Joel could get *really* nasty. Even when I was around. I was just a kid.'

'A kid? How many years ago are we talking?'

I shrugged. 'Twenty or something?'

'Twenty?'

'Yeah.'

'People mellow with age, mate.'

'I can't believe you're taking his side.'

'I just think, maybe, there's something else going on here. Do you see him as a father figure you want to lash out at?'

'Hey, don't joke. My father wasn't one of those old men who stand in pubs staring into space holding an eternal drink.'

'OK, now I'm thinking it's middle-aged men you have issues with. Do you see yourself potentially becoming Joel Brown? That's why you're keeping him at a distance. If you talk to him, you'll end up having a drink with him, then you'll be two old men, holding your eternal pint glasses, staring into the abyss together.'

'Shut it.'

'So did your dad own the whole building or what?'

'Yep, he was a property whizz. That's how he made his living. I used to help him out, carrying fridges, building things. Man, the things he could just *build* on his own. I didn't inherit any of those skills, mind you, just hammered nails where I was told.'

'How many properties did he have?' Bill asked with pound signs in his eyes.

'A few.'

Bill choked on his beer. 'Are you rich?'

'Nah. He didn't care enough about money.'

'Dammit. Talk about spoiling a good thing.'

'Yeah. He charged low rents, so the maths didn't quite work out and he gradually sold them off to make ends meet, except for the little place on the Archway Road. I was renting in Stroud Green when he died, so I moved into it, good size bachelor pad, and a room I use as an office. That financial ease enabled me to go part-time at the Met and start training up to work private.'

'Very nice,' Bill said. 'I commute from Carpenders Park every day.' He spoke about the eternal rise in house prices. I made sympathetic sounds. We bought more rounds. It was hard not to, positioned as we were, leaning on the bar. And things got blurrier.

I filled Bill in on what I knew about the Donsaw case and asked what he made of it all. I wouldn't do this with just anyone. Bill was a trusted confidante.

'He threatened the residents that he'd burn down the building, then a fire started on his roof terrace, and now we've got proof,' Bill said. 'He's in deep Brad.'

'All the neighbours really wanted him out,' I said.

'I wonder if they could have got together to plot this thing.'

'The mailbox was such a sorry sight,' I said. 'Makes me think they couldn't have got organised enough for that. But if one of those residents wanted to take it upon themselves... Would they risk burning down the building though?'

'Could have done some real damage.'

'I spoke to four sets of neighbours, and two of them used the phrase: *I don't want to repeat what Neddy said. This is the PG version.*'

Bill took one of his slow, steadying breaths. 'An unusual

phrase, suggesting they've spent time together, getting their story straight!'

'Alright,' I said. 'Don't get over-excited.'

'And those threats Neddy shouted at everyone would be enough to get a lot of protective parents into action. What are your thoughts on the other parents?'

'They seemed very... gentle.'

'That's the perfect cover now, isn't it? And the two that said *PG version* were less so?'

'They were angry.'

'Angry enough to scheme against Neddy?'

'Maybe.'

A smiling, glaze-eyed Bill started drumming on the bar. 'But maybe it was Neddy!'

I lowered my hand, gesturing he not yell. 'He was having a party up there with his mates. I hardly think that was the moment he decided to start a device to set his building aflame.'

'Unless it was calculated. He starts a fire, then creates evidence it was a careless accident.'

'Why bother making it seem like an accident if he's been threatening people all week?'

'To cover his arse when it comes to the law. He covered it well enough to con the fire department. Or one of the neighbours wanted him out, and complaining to the landlord — and the police — wasn't getting them anywhere. So they set up the device; either to get him into Brad with the police, or do away with him altogether.'

'But for them to risk harming the rest of the building?' I asked again. 'The culprit, if it was a resident, might have been alert to getting their own family and everyone else out, maybe after making sure the top flat was consumed. The way things have worked out, they couldn't have hoped for a better outcome.'

Bill raised an eyebrow. 'Is that a subtle way of asking me to check on criminal records on the rest of the residents?'

'I can't see any of our respectable Pond Square residents having done time.'

'Not *yet*,' Bill said. 'Or it could have been one of the party goers.'

'Yeah?'

'If this was an Agatha Christie, they'd all have a motive — a spurned lover; a music critic who can't stand Neddy's band, who actually had his own dreams of stardom that were dashed because he was told he had no musical talent; the governess of a small child whose death Neddy is responsible for, who has spent years living under an assumed identity waiting for the perfect moment to set Neddy's flat on fire, only for her entire life history to come to the surface in the final chapter...'

I realised how drunk Bill was then, but we bought another round. It was hard not to, what with our position, leaning on the bar.

4

My living room is a sixteen-by-thirteen feet space. Its main features include the stacks of books obscuring the whole of one wall, and a sofa bed — its dual features I use regularly, making the room a living room during the day and a bedroom at night. There's also an upright piano I can't play, and some nice antique things — including a circular oak table with chairs, a chesterfield armchair and a liberty lamp, which makes the room look like it belongs to a man of moderate means who's determined to enjoy the finer things in life. The reality is they were offerings from Joel's second-hand furniture shop downstairs, too convenient and good value to refuse.

The apartment also contains a miniature wet room and kitchen, where I usually sit on a stool at the counter to consume a sandwich or ready-made soup.

I awoke at dawn on the sofa bed, still in its sofa form, fully clothed, and feeling tender, to say the least. I didn't remember saying goodbye to Bill and I didn't remember arriving back at the flat.

I drank a glass of water, changed into a fresh T-shirt and

wandered around, expecting to see the manila envelope Bill had given me to appear at some point.

It didn't.

I searched with a more serious intent. Then I started to despair. My first full day on a case and I'd got shit-faced and lost a report. I bet even Sherlock on a nose full of snuff never had this happen.

I tore through the apartment until 10am, all the while getting pummelled by the thumping in my head, before relenting to the fact the report was likely not in the flat.

I jogged to The Woodman. I could see Rachel, the barmaid, through the pub window (I'd overheard her name the previous night at some point), young and hip, lipstick-red hair in a ponytail, black-framed harlequin glasses, tight jeans. I knocked on the glass and waved.

'We're not open!' she shouted, not looking very happy. Hopefully, her expression was due to the fact she had to work first thing in the morning and had nothing to do with me.

'I know!' I called back. I made a vague gesture with my arms that communicated I needed to get in anyway.

Rachel rolled her eyes and unlatched the door.

'Thanks, slight emergency. I think I left an A4 manila envelope in here yesterday. Pretty important. I'm having a shocker to tell the truth.'

'I tidied. There was no lost property. Only a few umbrellas.'

'Could I come in and look?'

'The place is spotless,' she said in a bored tone. 'I've cleaned everywhere and I didn't find anything.'

A wave of nausea made me sway as panic threatened to make me puke. I took a breath and heard myself beg, 'It's a work thing. Jobs are at stake. If I looked around, at least I can say I looked for it.'

She stepped aside.

I entered, made a beeline for last night's drinking stools. Nothing.

I couldn't call Bill and tell him I'd lost a classified report that wasn't supposed to leave his station. My old mates on the force did endless checks on my behalf. They had a soft spot for me. I was a tragic case whose only purpose left in life was to work cases. They knew I'd be useless without their help. So, the current arrangement was they never refused, and the mood was light, breezy and agreeable. We didn't talk about the magnitude of what I asked because if they thought about it, it was just so awful. If anyone was caught in the act... But what are the chances of being caught out when you're simply passing on information to your boring, responsible neighbourhood PI?

This was why I didn't drink. Usually. If I gave into that unsavoury pastime, that light, glazed mood, that subdued, amused consciousness, there'd be no coming back. Rachel would know my name the way I knew hers. She'd know my order. I'd have a regular stool at the bar, a face like Joel Brown's, and a pile of lost, confidential manila envelopes.

This thought process could have gone on, but I was thrown a lifeline. 'Why don't you ask Joel?' Rachel called out from behind the bar.

'Joel?'

'He helped you home last night.'

'Joel?'

'Yes. Old geezer, grey hair, acts like lord of the manor. He said he knew where you lived and he put your arm over his shoulder and carried you out of here.'

The Highgate Murder

The image was enough to make me light-headed. I had no memory of it, but it was a lead. I jogged home.

Our building had two entrances. The door to the left led to the two upstairs apartments. The door to the right was the door to Joel Brown's shop.

In my youth, it had been a bookshop, a lovely, musty, clustered old place. I never went in there on my own because Joel was such a beast, but when Pap had business there, he'd usually return with something pulpy from the crime section. I've never parted with those gifts, and now they're clustered against a wall on the floor above where they'd previously sat twenty years ago.

I guess second-hand books didn't cover the rent these days, so Joel now bought and sold second-hand furniture. The shop was cramped. Antique furniture had been adroitly piled in there, making maximum use of every inch of the space, as if by a skilled Tetris champion. The mustiness was still present.

At the heart of it sat Joel Brown, looking surprisingly dapper behind his desk. He had a portly frame but hid it well with a black shirt and dark blue blazer. This was something I noticed a lot of surviving rockers of the sixties did, become sharp dressers to counter balance the grizzled man within.

Even his ruddy face, which possessed a lion-like quality, like it was easily prone to a ferocious roar, was currently offset by a pair of Lennon glasses.

A Van Morrison song played on a vintage speaker. His eyes were fixed on a thin, battered copy of Philip Larkin.

'Still a bookshop owner at heart,' I said.

Joel looked up at me, deadpan. 'How do you mean?'

How did I mean? It was too early and I was in no state to answer such questions. But I tried. 'You... reading a book.'

The eyes flicked down to the book and back up at me. 'Yes. Yes, I suppose I am.'

'Listen, Joel. I have a vague recollection of last night, rambling something rude to anyone who walked past me.'

He put his book down and regarded me. He didn't confirm or deny what I'd said.

'Anyway, this is a bit awkward. I had a few too many ales last night and Rachel said you helped me. Home.'

Joel shrugged modestly. 'You needed a shoulder to lean on.'

'Well, thanks. You deserve some good karma there. I had a brown envelope with me with some work documents—'

Joel held up his hand and stopped me having to go through the whole sordid explanation. 'It's in your flat.'

'What?'

'The envelope you had with you, I brought it home with you last night. I was going to dump you on my sofa, but I felt in your pocket and found your key. I helped you up to your flat... You know, your hall light doesn't work.'

'Yeah, it's on my to-do list.'

Joel nodded. 'I brought the envelope and put it on the coffee table next to your sofa. I couldn't see a bed.'

'It's a sofa bed. You have to pull it out.'

'Ah.'

'Well, what can I say? Thanks a lot. I owe you one.'

'Call it a pint, now I know you're a patron of The Woodman. Two bachelors living together with a pub over the road—'

'We don't really live together, but... it's a deal.' I smiled, backing out of the shop, stung by the high cost of this good deed. 'Thanks again.'

. . .

BACK IN THE FLAT UPSTAIRS, the missing report was under the T-shirt I'd taken off and thrown on it a moment ago.

I collapsed in my armchair, looking at the envelope. I was reminded of the plot bomb in *Chinatown*, where JJ Gittes is told a key clue right at the start of the film, but he doesn't listen. He needs to take a hero's journey, drop his ego and arrogance, and by the end of the film he's told the same thing and realises its relevance.

Now I'd made my own 'hero's journey', humiliating myself all around the neighbourhood, and finally making my way back to my own coffee table. I could hear Gittes speak one of the film's great lines to me: 'This job takes a certain amount of finesse.'

Finesse was something I was certainly running short on.

I tore open the envelope and read the report. Beneath the dry police jargon, there wasn't much I didn't already know, and it didn't feel like great value for what I'd put myself through.

On the night of the fire, Neddy had had a party that went into the early hours. At some point in the night, everyone left for another location. At twenty minutes past 3am, a passer-by saw the flames and saved the day, just as Martin Ashi in Flat 4 had described. The police and fire engines arrived shortly thereafter. The house was evacuated and the fire dealt with.

All the residents were accounted for except for Neddy and Alex. The firefighters made a thorough search and were satisfied they weren't home.

The following day, Gavin Morgan from Flat 1 contacted the police to report Neddy's threatening behaviour and offer up the note Neddy had slipped into his mailbox. The police questioned the rest of the house and they confirmed the threats that had been made.

The police tried to speak to Neddy that day. He was aggressive and uncommunicative, so they took him in for formal questioning. He was evasive in his answers. He said there had been no harsh words exchanged with other tenants. When confronted with reports of what the other tenants had said, he shrugged and said they had it coming.

Concerning the fire, he said he'd had a barbecue on the roof and assumed that must have been the cause. The question was asked, could there have been a connection with the fire and his threats about starting a fire? On hearing this, Neddy became loud, aggressive and wouldn't answer any more questions without a lawyer. A lawyer arrived to say 'no' on his behalf.

There was a short profile on each resident. A fact that stood out was that Morgan was a lawyer. He'd been savvy enough to keep Neddy's threatening note for later presentation to the police. The reaction for a lot of people on receiving something so unpleasant might have been to throw it away. Also, Martin from Flat 4 was a landlord who owned other properties like my pap had. Perhaps, like Pap, he'd have a knack for making things.

It was interesting how badly Martin wanted to get up to the terrace after the fire to put a tarpaulin down. Perhaps a chance to make sure all ostensible evidence had been removed?

Reading and mulling over the report, the disconcerted feeling due to my idiotic morning had faded away. I was feeling more like a detective. I was able to sit at my desk. I even crossed my feet on it.

I could imagine that none of this would have got as far as it had if Neddy could have spoken to the police calmly. But I could understand Donsaw's concern. If I was on a jury and a lawyer delivered this evidence well, Neddy could end up doing time. Now I'd looked into it further and had found evidence there had been a fire-starting device, it was even more serious.

I WONDERED if I'd have better luck trying to communicate with the boy at the centre of all this. I'd tried calling Neddy throughout the previous day but he never picked up, so I drove Merkel, the Mini, to the address Alex had given me.

Neddy had moved only a few streets further down the hill, to Archway. He must have been a fan of the neighbourhood. Archway used to be part of Highgate. At some point in its history, the old-world charm had been torn down to make way for a modern, concrete sprawl. Further up the hill, Highgate avoided a similar fate due to successful protests. Maybe because this new, ugly area was so different from the rest of Highgate, it got its own name — Archway. It took the name from a bridge you drove under as you entered the area — like an 'archway'. The bridge itself is morbidly known as suicide bridge, and a spiky safety fence runs along the top to deter jumpers. I remembered driving with Pap here, him telling me the grim history. I made some monosyllabic comment like, 'Oh, cool.' I have a lot of memories of Pap waxing lyrical, and me nodding without words, perhaps without thoughts outside of what was happening in my world of novels and TV shows. I can't have been great company.

Despite everything I just said about the smoky artery of Archway's central thoroughfare, I discovered its back streets were quiet havens of Victorian housing, lined with plane trees and BMWs. I wondered what it was about quiet, cookie-cutter streets that appealed to this edgy rocker. I also wondered what his relationship with the new neighbours was like.

I found number 67. No one answered my initial knock. I tried again and triggered the yap of a dog. An angry voice shouted for it to shut up.

I knocked some more. The dog barked some more, and a young, unhappy man in his late twenties opened the door. The sides of his head were shaved, the long black mass on top was slimed back. His hooded eyes were far apart, making his face snake-like and mean. They looked me up and down, weighing me for a fight. Under six foot, in a dark blue tracksuit, his stance was unnecessarily wide.

I sensed this was Neddy.

'*Yeah*?'

'Neddy?'

'Who wants to know?'

'I've been hired to help your lawyer over the fire.'

A confused sneer. 'What fire?'

'Pond Square.'

'What's it to you?'

I resisted pointing out I'd just told him. 'I'm a private investigator. You're in pretty deep with the police, maybe more than you know. I need to find any evidence I can of your innocence and a chat with you would be a good start.'

He stared at me with big, crazy eyes. It struck me as affected, contriving to intimidate me with a ferociousness that boarded on insanity. I tried again. 'Could you help me out here?'

'Why don't you fuck off?' were the words he finally blessed me with, and that was the PG version.

I resisted rolling my eyes. If he wasn't going to help me, I'd ask him something I was curious about. 'Edward Donsaw hired me to help you. Do you know who that is?'

Neddy just carried on burning his stare into me. If this kid wasn't going to help himself and land himself in prison out of pure fat-headedness, maybe I was wrong about the insanity angle.

Then a single, not particularly loud bark came from behind him. It sounded like it came from a young pup, and the pup became the object of Neddy's vitriol. 'Shut the *fuck* up!' he shouted over his shoulder.

The pup reacted with a succession of louder barks.

'I said: *shut up!*'

The pup barked louder. Neddy turned his back on me and stormed down his hallway to where I could see a little black dog with long, floppy ears.

Neddy roared at it to shut up, getting the dog more excited. It looked like a battle of wits that could go on for some time. Then Neddy smacked it across the face.

I could feel my blood get hot. 'Why don't you treat your dog better?' I called down the corridor.

Now he was coming at me with a fighter's swagger. I was hoping he'd try to hit me, but he halted and hissed, 'What did you say?'

I told him.

'Who do you think you are?'

'A human being,' I said. 'That's why I try to act like one.'

A lot of playground language started flying at me. He might have hurt my feelings if I were a nine-year-old.

I didn't feel like backing down, so I stood there and took it until he finally slammed the door in my face. That started the dog barking again, and that started Neddy barking again.

I was going to ask if he knew anyone who might want to set fire to him, but the answer was clear — anyone who'd had the good fortune to meet him.

5

My blood was up and I wasn't sure if it would ever come down again. I drove home, made a cup of tea and got online. It occurred to me that I'd done a general web search for Neddy after Donsaw had led me to believe he was well known, but I hadn't looked within the social media realm.

It didn't take long to find Neddy and his band doing their own marketing. I had to laugh at them, scowling at me through the screen. I could imagine them in front of the photographer. 'Sneer! Meaner! Now give me a really sexy scowl.'

The band was *Nucleomara*. I checked their website and saw they had a gig in the Dublin Castle that evening. I also got a visual and names on all the band members. I'd found my *in*. Maybe I could infiltrate his inner circle to get some kind of handle on the little thug.

With nothing to do for the proceeding few hours, I called detective sergeant Kim Palmer, another friend in the Met. I didn't want to speak to Bill, didn't want to hear any anecdotes about the previous evening.

'Hello?' she answered with a hint of disbelief.

'It's Mike.'

'Nice to hear from you, punk.'

'Is this a good time?'

'It's a perfectly good time. Are you going to ask me on a date?'

'What?'

'I heard you took Bill out for a drink in Highgate last night. What am I, chopped liver?'

'I wish.'

'Where've you been hiding?'

'Just focused on work. That's what's working for me right now.'

The banter had been fast and furious, for me anyway, causing me to blurt out that line. The words sounded stiff, even to me.

But Kim didn't miss a beat. 'What you working on?'

'Fire in Highgate village. I got Bill up here for a little forensic action. He brought me some basic info for the case.'

'Really?' Kim said. 'That's against protocol.'

'It's okay,' I said. 'I bribed him.'

'Oh. Okay.'

'This character, Neddy Mara, is at the centre of it all and he won't speak to me. He's got no official record, but I'm sure he's on the system.'

'Do I get a bribe?'

'Um... no.'

'Any idea what's going on?'

'My client's theory is, he's a rockstar and some jealous people might be out to frame or hurt him. Transpires, the band hasn't gone beyond gigging in pubs. And I met the kid. He's crazy enough for arson, and enough of a bastard that anyone who's met him would want him to burn alive. So really, it's wide open.'

'How did he upset Mr Laid-back?'

'I'm too angry to tell you right now.'

'This is you angry?'

'I'm fuming.'

'Got your work cut out for you.'

'Yeah, it's great. My client said there's bad blood in the family, so there's another angle; not to mention any animal lovers out there.'

'What do you mean?'

Again, her quick-fire delivery caused me to speak before thinking. I really had to start training myself to pause. 'I went to his address because he never answers his phone, and it was only down the road. He had a puppy and was abusing it.'

'What?'

'Smacked it hard across the face, tiny little thing.'

'Tell me where he lives, I'll sort him out.'

'You can do that?'

'What am I? A pub landlord? Yes, I can. I don't know why you didn't report him yourself.'

We had to follow Kim's moral compass now. I resigned myself; we were officially off track. 'That's how people act,' I said. 'I accept it.'

I heard her sigh. 'Mike, it's not as bad as all that.'

'Isn't it?'

'Listen, Mike. Something beyond awful happened to you and I don't know if this career of yours is the best way to move on. Everyone has good and bad in them. It's not much, but I think of myself as a source for good. Every day I try to make a bit of a difference. There's a lot of good in the world, and right at the top of that list are puppies. This lowlife is abusing one and I'm going to sort it out. How's that for balance?'

'Okay,' I said. 'I didn't mean to play the hopeless card. I had a few drinks last night.'

The last line was an attempt to hear what Bill might have said about the evening, but Kim didn't bite. 'Don't *I* get a drink?' she said.

'If you do something about that dog, you get a packet of crisps.'

'I'll take your crisps and raise you a poker game. I'm getting the gang together on Monday night and you're coming. No excuses.'

'Poker?'

'Yes.'

'One of those poker nights that go on forever because no one can remember the rules?'

'That's why it's hilarious. The guys need it after a day in uniform.'

I harrumphed for lack of a better answer.

'I'll take a look at your thing later on today and give you a call back.'

'Promises promises,' I said.

I GRABBED a bagel and a cup of tea from Ivanka's cafe, an incongruous gem of a place a few doors down from me. Amongst the grim kebab grills, musty thrift shops and greasy spoons, was a tiny room run by a Ukrainian couple. They played up to the vintage charm of the surrounding area, with black and white pictures of the village on the wall, and a medley of weathered furniture they could very well have picked up from Joel Brown's shop.

Ivanka waited on tables upstairs, always with a smile

and good conversation. She'd take your order and walk down a narrow staircase, to where her partner did all the cooking. They worked all day, seven days a week. If you timed it right, you'd see them walking home in the evening, arm in arm, down the Archway Road.

My phone buzzed, Kim's number. I smiled a thank you to Ivanka and took my tea to a bench outside the cafe.

'Hit me.'

'Excuse me?'

'*Hit* me.'

'What are you, Mike Hammer?'

'I wasn't being Mike Hammer. It was an apt thing to say.'

'I would lose that.'

'Jeez, okay. Did you find out anything interesting, please?'

Kim sighed. 'I shouldn't encourage you, but it's pretty interesting stuff. His mother's deceased, one Catherine Moore, suicide, a year ago.'

'Flipping heck.'

'That's no excuse for how he treats that innocent dog.'

'I didn't say anything about the dog. I was just exclaiming surprise, and sympathy.'

'I'm not letting him off the hook so easily. Anyway, Catherine Moore. Do you know who I'm talking about?'

'Should I?'

'She was a showbiz type, had an acting career, a bit of a music career. I think she was mostly known for her... um... heaving bosoms.'

'I was always more of a leg man.'

'I'll have to remember that. Also, Neddy seems to have changed his name by deed poll. His name was originally Neddy O'Mara. He's the son of Derek O'Mara.'

'Derek O'Mara, I've heard of him,' I said, keeping my voice level.

'I thought you might have, your old man being a notorious character of the infamous Square Mile.'

'Kim, the Square Mile is specifically and only *the City*, aka the financial quarter and the business that goes on there.'

'Soho's a square mile.'

'But it's the City that's referred to as the Square Mile. Your comment infers my father was a legendary futures trader or hedge fund manager.'

'Ugh. Okay. You got me. *I thought you might have heard of Derek O'Mara, your old man being a player in Soho back in the day.*'

'Sure, I know *of* him. This explains a lot. Neddy is the son of a tough guy who intimidates, gets his way and runs the show. The plot thickens!'

'Be careful, Mike Hammer. I don't want anything happening to you.'

'Thanks, Kim. You've been a big help.'

'Poker is on. I'll text you details.'

'That was quick. Having a busy day at work, are we?'

'Not too busy to help *you* out.'

SHE RANG OFF, and I sat back against the windowpane of Ivanka's cafe. I could hear my heart beating in my chest over the sound of traffic on the Archway Road.

Derek O'Mara.

He was a Soho player from my pap's generation. They'd both owned clubs a stone's throw from each other. It was likely they crossed paths. Pap never mentioned his name. I first heard of him when I was in the Met. He was mostly legal these days, a respectable elder statesman but well connected, and he didn't take kindly to being disturbed. From what I heard, if his name ever came up in an investigation, coppers did everything they could to work around him unless the situation was critical.

I rushed home and searched through my box files until I found my father's old address book. Large, hardback and scarlet, inside was a lifetime of contacts, hand-written in his neat penmanship.

I made a list of four contacts I thought might be useful and texted their numbers, saying I was working a case and wanted to talk to O'Mara.

Then I got online and looked up Catherine Moore. Her career had happened so long before the digital age, there wasn't much of an online presence for her, just a very basic wiki page and a few obituaries. She studied theatre from a young age, then had a career in television for over a decade that seemed to end when motherhood would have begun. She'd also released two pop albums during her showbiz years that charted in the UK.

The online images were only of a young Catherine, dark haired and dark eyed, with a dimpled smile and chipmunk cheeks.

Very pretty.

Dead now.

I looked at different images of her for longer than I should have until an unbearable depression started sinking into me.

Meeting Neddy had depressed me. Maybe living in Highgate village was softening me. Much worse things were happening out there in the world. But that was the thing. Neddy was such an average berk, and that was how he acted when you got a glimpse into his front hall. It was enough to make a man live like Raymond Chandler — writing stories about lonely detectives, then drinking yourself to death.

Then the chat with Kim had depressed me further. I guess I'd always had a thing for her. She was so lovely, and whenever she highlighted that loveliness, it reminded me of what I didn't have. Then I felt like a scumbag for having such thoughts.

I found myself in the bathroom. In the cabinet lived different bottles of pills. When I became a widower, I'd been prescribed a lot of sleeping pills. It comforted me to have them in the flat. If I swallowed enough of them, there'd be no more thinking, no more Neddys of the world, no more Kim or marital memories.

A counsellor I'd been sent to recommended journaling and that was something I'd found helpful. It had got me this far. That and the work. The two were combined really because I wrote about the cases. I'd written about all of them; all but one — one I don't think or talk about and only refer to in my mind as the Incident.

It helped me flesh out ideas and make connections.

I left the bathroom, picked up my journal and scribbled away the afternoon until I felt halfway human again.

It all centred around Neddy.

Was this a kid who would set up a device that could burn down a building with families inside? I didn't see why not. The suicide of a mother was enough of an explanation for that madness. Unnatural loss affects us all in different ways. Having my wife taken from me so violently was near unbearable.

My ruminations were disturbed by a text. Steve Korona, an old friend of my father's I'd just texted, said he'd be delighted to see me. I knew I wouldn't get away with a phone call and braced myself to be invited to one of his haunts.

And it was time to go to work. I used a hair trimmer to rid my face of its beard, then found an old razor in the back of a cupboard and gave myself a proper shave. I pulled an old, grey beanie down low over my head and put a pair of black-framed glasses on. I was in disguise and ready for a night at the Dublin Castle.

6

I took the tube to Camden to avoid getting stuck in traffic. A ten-minute walk up Parkway, past the Jazz Cafe, a favourite haunt of Pap's he used to take me to. It didn't have many jazz gigs these days as they were trying to appeal to the paying public, but they'd kept the name.

I arrived at the Dublin Castle, a legendary place, originally built for Irish labourers working on the London railways. The idea was that keeping nationalities segregated would lead to less violence. It became a music venue where the likes of Madness and Amy Winehouse started out. And it was always crammed, a rare place in London that attracted all types and ages; they kept it real by not upping the price of the beer.

It was a building of aesthetic contrasts. Elegant, with long, arched, keystone windows, intricate overhang along the top and square quoins running down its sides, painted white with pink-red trim, like a strawberry cup cake, and grungy revellers always milling outside, smoking and drinking.

Glasses, beanie and beardless, it was still imperative I

avoided Neddy. If we bumped into each other head on, he'd recognise me and lord knows what the little nut bag would do.

It was nine o'clock. I could hear sounds like cars crashing as I entered and, at the back of the Castle, I could see the band on stage, Neddy working his guitar and head banging with the same intensity I'd seen him do everything else.

The singer, eyes shut tight, roared into a mic he gripped with both hands. Intermittently, the grating of guitar would abruptly stop and a Mariah Carey-like pop chorus would happen, then cars would start crashing again.

I hovered around the bar, at the front end of the pub, as far from Neddy — and the stage — as possible, and bought myself a much-needed pint. The Dublin Castle and the music were making me feel old. This was a place I'd snuck into when I was a fourteen-year-old, underaged drinker — I did the maths — twenty years ago. Good god.

The kid behind the bar looked a little weary too. I nodded at the stage. 'What is this?'

The barman smiled as he poured me a pint. '*Metalcore*,' he answered dryly. Good to know it wasn't just me, or it could have been the barman was clever at measuring and bonding with customers.

He set the drink in front of me.

'I'll have another,' I said. 'I'll sink this one while you're pouring.'

'Good plan,' the barman answered.

I downed a healthy dose of my second pint and felt rewardingly fuzzy. I reminisced to distract myself, a blond piano player, a small basement gig in Soho. The more I drank, the easier it was to transport myself from the Dublin

The Highgate Murder

Castle to the small Soho basement where I first saw the blond piano player.

~

A LITTLE PLACE just off Carnaby Street, through a door and down some steps, to a venue the size of my living room. Atmosphere was provided by dim hanging bulbs, candles glowing in jars on each small table and red curtains draped behind the stage.

Having a beer with my old man, we'd just had a bite to eat at a new place next door, trendy British cuisine: steak and kidney pie, sausage and mash, fish finger sandwiches, presented daintily at inflated prices. Pap was very amused by the food of his youth getting a rebranding.

I don't think I knew what we were going to see. Pap had probably told me to keep the date in the diary and who was performing, and I'd not listened to the latter part.

We'd seen jazz quintets play at the venue, which was comical, squashed in a corner like the deftly packed furniture in Joel Brown's shop, trying not to take each other's eyes out with their instruments.

It was fitting as (so Pap had told me) iconic bands of the sixties like the Stones started their careers in these very basements of Soho, standing on sets of milk crates to elevate themselves above the twenty-person crowd.

Pap went to buy beers at the tiny bar at the back of the room. I read the venue's flyer that was lying on the table. A singer-pianist was performing. Then she arrived, took off a denim jacket and sat down at the piano. She was wearing a perfectly fitting, sleeveless, black dress with white polka dots, her mane of hair falling down her back.

She had an old-fashioned, bluesy style to whatever she

played, like how Nina Simone had an elegant, classical style, even when she sang the blues.

I never got lost in the music like Pap. Those offbeat melodies and broken chords just killed him. But this singer had me transfixed. She sang songs from the canon in an unbelievably sexy voice, low and heavy. And a legendary blues singer had just died, so she played a lot of his songs in her own cool, easy style.

She finished her first set. It didn't take long for her to acknowledge every member of the applauding audience with a smiling glance. Pap and I sat to her immediate left, in line to get the last glance. I could hear my heart pounding like a Gene Krupa drum solo, to use one of Pap's phrases.

Our eyes met and something happened, that movie moment. What I was feeling was surely showing on my face. This moment would cause me embarrassment for years to come, as it was all happening in front of Pap. 'I'm going to the bar,' I said. He'd not seen me in that mode before, I must have looked like a shark. An amused, knowing grin on his face, he tapped his beer bottle, indicating it was half full. 'Nothing for me,' he said.

I was nervous now, setting myself up for an embarrassing rejection in front of my own pap. But I had a plan. I was going to complement her on the set, then buy her a drink, then... see where things went from there. It wasn't much of a plan, but it was a plan.

The piano player was standing at the bar. It wasn't much of a bar. A woman was serving drinks behind a foot-long counter in a space the size of a closet, another person to closely witness me get egg on my face.

'Great set,' I said.

The piano player smiled. Her eyes were hazel with

golden flecks. 'Thanks,' she said in a singer's voice, melodious even in conversation.

The barmaid brought her a glass of red wine. The piano player handed over a musician's token.

'Oh. I wanted to buy you a drink.' I'd said it instinctively. It was the biggest blessing of my life. Because if I hadn't blurted it out, I'd have come up with nothing else. What else was there to say? But I'd said my line, and she said, 'Stick around after the set if you like and I'll give you another chance.'

I RETURNED TO MY SEAT. Pap has his lips pursed, trying not to crack up. 'Alright?'

'Yes,' I answered sharply.

'Didn't you get yourself a drink?'

I realised I hadn't and we shared a chuckle.

I looked at the flyer again to read her name. Alison May.

She acknowledged the audience again at the end. I told Pap I was going to stick around. He put on his coat with an amused leer. 'Don't stay out too late.'

'I won't,' I said, feeling like a kid not wanting his father to embarrass him at the school gates.

Alison May took care of some admin with the venue staff, and we left together, exchanged names, and embarked on a ten-hour date.

Soho was relatively quiet on a mid-week evening. We had a drink at the John Snow, talked about music. I told her about Pap, what a diehard jazz fan he was and how I grew up in smoky clubs, catching legends like Lionel Hampton and Anita O'Day at the back end of their careers. Pap ran a beloved Soho club called La Roca, and for years after his club-owning days were behind him, he still got preferential treatment in local music venues, like a good table. I only realised when I was older they didn't usually allow young children into these places.

We walked a couple of blocks and had another drink at the Blue Posts. She told me she was carving out a career as a musician and how it enabled her to travel. The more she talked, the more I saw past the diamond-shaped face and glowing hair, the more I relaxed and was myself.

I told her I wasn't happy with where my career was going. After putting my time in as a uniformed police officer, I'd been told I had a talent for face recognition and was pigeon holed into Vido — a career watching videos for a living; private cameras, smart phone footage, CCTV, anything we could get our hands on to help on cases. I'd dutifully put my time in there too, but higher forces were blocking my efforts to advance my career. Apparently, I had a gift for spotting faces and delivering results fast. I was put into an elite team of screen watchers known as Super Recognisers.

Another drink at the Coach and Horses. They called last orders. Alison told me her friends were working in the French House. They'd let us in and we could keep drinking.

Her two girlfriends, working the bar, were happy to see her. The place was buzzing with old actor lovies and Alison was surprised they all knew me.

La Roca was in the heart of theatreland and actors I recognised from TV would often know Pap and talk to us whenever he was walking me through the neighbourhood. Some of these actors were TV detectives. Lieutenant Dempsey and DS Makepeace stopped and had a chat with us once, a big moment for young Mike Seferis.

That faded off as the years went by and the cast of well-known actors of the day changed and no longer knew who my father was. But the French House was a hub for the old guard, silver-tongued and silver-haired, slapping me on the back and asking after 'good old Nick'.

Everyone treated me and Alison like a couple which was thrilling for me.

She revealed she was a north Londoner like myself. We lived a blessedly close distance from each other. We'd later joke the relationship worked because it was so geographically convenient.

She lived in Finsbury Park with a girlfriend, and I was sharing a flat in Stroud Green with Patchy, my friend and colleague.

Dawn broke. We left the French House and rode a couple of Boris bikes up to our neighbourhood for morning kebabs.

We rode from there to her place, walked up some stairs, collapsed on a bed and held onto each other for dear life until my alarm went off an hour later. She lent me a pair of sunglasses and I dragged myself into work to stare at video screens for the rest of the day.

The office cracked up at the sight of me, immensely hungover, in a pair of shades, holding a bottle of water with both hands I couldn't even bring myself to take small sips from. But something got me through that morning. The blond piano player said she wanted to see me again. I had her number. All I had to do was not die that morning.

Pap was very pleased when I revealed all later. 'That firecracker?' he asked. It was a memory that still made me smile, despite how it all ended.

∽

Now I was here — a very different kind of evening. I

thought about the character I had to be if I was going to get anywhere in this case. That was part of the appeal of this job, going undercover to find out what I needed to know. Nobody knew what I was up to. People only saw an illusion of me. Getting out of myself that way, that was how I kept pushing on.

I took a long slug of beer and signalled to the barman for a third drink. He laughed. I think he liked my style.

The set went on mercilessly longer than I expected. I lost count of the beers I downed.

Neddy got off the stage where a groupie was waiting for him. She was heavily done up with lips like a carp, brown hair piled on her head, tight white jeans and a baggy, knit jumper that hung off one shoulder. He clamped his hand on her butt, and they exchanged conversation and open-mouth kisses. Likely, this was the girlfriend, Jane.

The boyish-faced bassist came to the bar to exchange a band token for a beer. I waited until he got his drink, then approached and thanked him for a great set, hoping he'd be more human than Neddy. Having seen their website, I knew this was Jude Pope.

'Thanks, mate,' he said, and I sighed inwardly with relief. His voice and manner were actually appreciative and gentle. His pretty-boy looks and floppy hair made him look like a young sixties rocker before the years had taken their toll.

'How long have you guys been together?'

'A few years now,' he said.

'Any albums out yet?'

'Nah, just a demo.'

'No record deal? I thought you guys were signed-up, jobbing musicians.'

The Highgate Murder

Jude laughed. 'You deserve a drink for that.' He called to the bartender. 'Mate! A couple of slammers.'

The barman poured two double-shots of yellowish liquid from a bottle with a label that read *alcoholic spirit*. We downed them. It tasted alcoholic.

'I wish,' Jude said. I had to backtrack in my mind to pick up our thread of conversation. 'In the daytime, I sell pizza. Keany, drums, just opened up a sandwich place in Chalk Farm.'

'I'm sensing a catering theme, here.'

'Chow and music,' Jude said. 'What else do you need?'

I held up my beer in a toast of agreement, then I prodded, 'What about the rest of the guys?'

'Nathan, vocals, is an electrician. Neddy, guitar...' He paused. 'I'm not sure.'

'He's the mysterious one,' I said.

Jude laughed.

'He looks familiar,' I said. 'Has he played in other bands?'

Jude shrugged. 'A couple, I think, maybe. None of them made it out of the Camden circuit.'

'He's got the groupies.' I nodded at the stage, where I was keeping Neddy in my peripheral. 'I've met her before. Jane, isn't it?'

Jude laughed. 'That's how she sees herself, a real Jane Birkin.'

'She's got the looks, Serge has got the talent?'

'Something like that,' Jude said. 'I better get back. Let's have one for the road.'

We shared another dose of *alcoholic spirit*. I slapped Jude on the back, giving him a cue to leave. I'd spotted Jane approaching and positioned myself to intercept her approach to the bar. Jude and Neddy were getting back on stage. I braced myself for what they had in store for their second set.

'Alright!' I smiled at Jane like we were old friends. 'Get you a drink?' Before she could protest, I explained, 'I'm mates with Jude. You're Jane, right?'

'Yeah,' she said, guarded.

'What you drinking?'

She hesitated for a moment. 'Gin and kiba.'

I repeated her order to the barman, hoping he wouldn't ask me what it was. I watched him pour gin, banana juice and cherry juice into a glass. Kids.

I also ordered a couple more 'slammers' on the off chance she'd accept one and let it loosen her tongue a bit. To talk. I handed one to her. 'It's how I introduce myself to people.'

Her aura wasn't exactly warm, but she accepted her red and yellow drink, and the double shot, and I raised mine in a toast. 'I'm Nick!' I shouted in her ear. The band had started up again.

'Cheers,' she shouted in my ear, piercing my ear drum. We downed the slammers. Her swollen features twitched. I chased the sour taste of the shot with beer.

'I heard about the fire last week!' I said.

The bond of drinking the shot had brought down her defences a bit, and the mention of the fire got her positively animated. 'Oh my god! It was the scariest thing ever.'

We exchanged words by leaning in and shouting into each other's ear. 'Was it a big one?' I asked. 'The party, I mean, not the fire.'

'Not at all!' she shouted, like her answer was a revelation. 'It was just me and the boys having a barbecue. He had an amazing view of London from up there. Now they've kicked him out.'

I shook my head in disgust. *Bastards.* 'How long have you and Neddy been together?'

Her eyes narrowed. 'A couple of years,' she said in the same tone of voice as her first words to me.

I blindsided her with flattery. 'He's awesome. He's going to the top. They're *tight*. I know a bunch of future superstars when I see it.'

'You think so?'

'With Neddy on guitar, I guarantee it. That's an amazing guitar he's got too. He must be loaded.'

Jane flinched. If I hadn't bought her a drink, she may have walked off then. 'He's got money, but he's had a hard life,' she said. 'Music is his escape.'

'Oh, sorry to hear that. That's probably why he's got the gift. You can learn technique and all that, but it takes a bit of suffering for the soul to grow.'

'Exactly.'

'What happened?'

'His mum killed herself not long ago.'

'Whoa, that's heavy. Was it out of the blue or what?'

'Yeah, it seemed to take everyone by surprise.'

'Were they close?'

She looked angry now. I guess a double *alcohol spirit* will only go so far. She took a deep breath and decided to go on. 'Didn't really see her when she was alive, that I knew of.'

'What about his father?'

'He doesn't talk about his parents,' she said with finality, causing an awkward silence. Well, awkward anyway; I wished it could have been silent. I nodded affably and shouted in her ear I'd see her around.

She spun on her heel and took her red and yellow drink back to her groupie location near the stage. I was about to make an immediate exit but waited to get the barman's attention so I could say goodbye. I caught his eye. 'Cheers, mate.'

He made me pause with a pointed finger and put two glasses on the bar. He poured us both one more measure of *alcoholic spirit*. Ceremony.

I felt ecstatic to get outside, away from *Nucleomara,* and wanted to hold on to the booze buzz. Lightweight that I was, I may well have been absolutely smashed at that point.

I got a couple of large cans of lager from a cornershop, drank on the train and sobbed silently. I must have been a sight. And The Woodman is right next door to Highgate station's exit. I may have decided I wanted another beer at that point, gone into The Woodman, and been not particularly polite to Rachel.

I may have had more to drink, and may have received a few concerned or disapproving glances. I may have seen Joel and said, 'I owe you a bloody pint, do I? Come on, then.'

I may even have started blabbing about Neddy, his mother and his dog. Or it may all have been an alcohol-induced dream. Because then the blond piano player was there, then Kim and Jane, all looking at me with concerned or disapproving glances for asking too many questions.

7

For the second morning running, I awoke on my sofa without remembering how I'd got there. When the pounding in my head was just about bearable, I pulled myself up for a cup of tea and a couple of aspirin. I could feel the sandpaper itch of next-day stubble on my face, an unpleasant sensation I hadn't felt in a long time. I promised myself a shave. As soon as I was able to get around to it.

I looked out the window. The day was overcast but bright enough to need a pair of sunglasses. I pulled on some fresh clothes, descended the stairs, and looked through Joel's shop window to see him sedentary at his desk with his nose in another book of poetry.

I knocked on the window. He waved me in. 'Morning, Joel.'

'It's my twin!' Joel replied.

'Excuse me?'

'We're wearing the same thing.'

I looked him up and down. Dark jeans and a black shirt. I couldn't argue.

'Just don't go around the neighbourhood ruining my reputation,' he said.

I didn't have an argument for that either.

'Just winding you up, son.'

I felt an inner wince at his term of endearment, but smiled at his hilarious wind up. 'Joel, I have a half memory of wandering into The Woodman last night.'

'Your half memory is correct.'

I felt the blood drain from my face. I'd been more certain than not I'd dreamt it. 'Was it carnage?'

'Ha-ha, two nights running I've seen you walk on your knuckles.'

'I guess I was still drunk from the night before.'

'You don't stay in shape, that's your problem.'

'What?'

'You're out of practice. A drop of the good stuff each day would stop it having such a devastating effect on you.'

'Oh, I get you. I'm fine if I stick to beer. Whisky hits me hard.'

'You were drinking vodka.'

'Vodka too.'

'You don't look as much of a wreck as I thought you would.'

'I can hide it well,' I said, feeling very green on the inside.

'I can do that too. Get to my chair, focus on my book, and customers are none the wiser I feel like a pig has shat in my head.'

'Thanks for the imagery. You can really read with a hangover?'

'I've never been so hungover I've been unable to read.'

I nodded, impressed. 'How did I make it home?'

'I escorted you.'

'Again?'

Joel shrugged. 'It's getting easier. I know what pocket you keep your key in now.'

'What... was I doing? ...in the pub.'

'You were leaning on the bar, buying a few drinks for people who were near you. You were telling me about a friend of yours, a kid who's gone off the rails. You were saying his mother had died?'

'Good grief.'

'What's the matter?'

'Just that... it wasn't the most appropriate thing for me to be sharing.'

'It's good to hear people caring about others—'

'Listen,' I cut in, backing out the door. 'Thanks for the escort.' My legs felt unsteady where they were and I needed to get them moving. 'I'll make sure I stay home tonight so I don't make it three nights in a row.'

'Or you can drop in on me, if you want to talk,' Joel said, halting my exit. 'You can see I'm not rushed off my feet here.'

'It's a deal,' I said, finally getting out of there.

I WALKED down the Archway Road, a cacophony of car horns, bus fumes and gaggles of people waiting at each bus stop.

I was angry with myself. Since moving into the upstairs flat, I'd diligently kept well away from Joel Brown. There'd been a couple of unavoidable interactions, and I'd nod to him in the street. I usually stayed away from The Woodman, after seeing him in there a couple of times, but convenience, and getting smashed in the Dublin Castle, had pulled me back in there.

Now he was telling me I could *drop in* on him if I wanted to talk. What else had I said last night that might have caused him to make that offer? I was less worried about details about the case and more concerned about anything I may have said about my own life. And where did he get off saying that? I wasn't a stranger. I knew him. I didn't buy it, the volatile curmudgeon I'd once known now talking about how good it was to hear about *caring about others*. Sure, people can mellow with age, but I don't buy into the idea of complete personality transplants.

Then again, what was happening to *me*, a drunk, rambling at people in a pub and having no idea what I may have said? I'd never had such an eventful evening that had just dropped out of my mind.

I'd been holding it together. I couldn't allow myself to lose control, and that meant no boozing, even if doing it as part of the job was my excuse. Otherwise, I may just spin apart completely.

I passed under suicide bridge. It was time to decide where I was going. I pulled out my phone and looked up Neddy's band. I followed the virtual thread of Keany, the drummer and sandwich seller. A couple of clicks and I found him publicising his sandwich shop on Chalk Farm Road. That sounded like a wholesome place to go, unlikely to be serving complimentary shots of alcoholic spirit.

It was a long shot, whether he'd be working so early after a gig at the Castle the night before. But Chalk Farm was a straight, longish walk down the hill, just what I needed to blow the cobwebs away.

I walked down Junction Road, turned onto Prince of Wales, and down Haverstock Hill into Chalk Farm. I passed the Round House, an old circular building where maybe trains used to be fixed, or at least spun around — hence the shape of the building. It became a seminal rock venue in the sixties or seventies, because the Beatles, or the Stones, or Bowie, played there — trivia courtesy of my old man.

Just beyond Marine Ices was a pleasant run of cafes and shops. The strip had been neglected for a long time, but as the popularity of Camden market became more and more stratospheric, its overflow was reaching further up to Chalk Farm.

Between a Vietnamese restaurant and a kitchen cabinet workshop was *Crisp Sandwiches*. The facade publicised 'Beer and Booze', but I was sure at this time of day their speciality was hot tea — a cup of which I needed badly.

Keany's cafe was long and narrow, and very rustic-chic. Wood was everywhere, the floors, the dark furniture that looked homemade, the crusty frames on the walls, the walls themselves. Old wine crates had been nailed flat to the walls so their sides served as shelves for crockery, napkins and a small library.

A group of three young men were drinking early beers at a table at the far end. Keany himself was behind a counter at the front of the cafe, a very cool cat, side burns the length of his face and his long brown hair in a man bun.

I hadn't eaten yet, and I ordered a braised beef (and crisps) sandwich with a cup of tea. So, it wasn't just a quirky restaurant name. I used to put crisps in my sandwiches at school. I'd never thought of paying someone to do it for me.

He started preparing it and I played my card. 'Don't I recognise you?'

He looked me up and down and shook his head. Dead expression, he was probably suffering a similar morning as me.

I made a face like I was doing long division in my head. 'Do you play in a band or something?'

His face lit up, just a little. 'Yeah.'

'Yeah, I've seen you guys around. *Nucleomara*, right?'

'Yeah, that's me.' He sliced through thick focaccia and pulled out some of the innards to make room for the fillings.

'That's weird. I've been following you guys for a while. You really have something, a real rock 'n' roll band.'

'Thanks.' He nodded, like the praise was unsurprising and deserved, quite a contrast to Jude's modest reaction.

'Is the life as rock 'n' roll as it looks? Backstage brawls, punch ups...?'

Keany shrugged. 'Pretty much, we have some big egos in the band.'

'Neddy?' I asked.

Now I had Keany smiling. 'What makes you say that?'

'I got that impression.'

'Oh yeah?'

'And I've had a conversation with him.'

That got a chuckle. 'We could make it big, but there's not a chance with him around. If any label were interested, Neddy's liable to punch their representative in the face. We even told him we want him out, but he won't listen.'

'Hold on, you're saying you fired him and he wasn't having it?'

'Exactly, didn't want to listen to what we were saying, still came to rehearsal, and he's still in the band.'

'That's crazy. I heard his mother died recently.' I waited for a solemn nod before continuing. 'Could that be the reason for his anger issues?'

'I knew him before, and I can tell you, it's by no means made him any more or less of an arsehole.'

'How did he get in the band?'

'Good musician. Only now we realise it's not worth it.'

'Does he ever mellow out?'

The Highgate Murder

'Nope.' He popped open a packet of Walkers and emptied it onto the open sandwich.

'I heard he started a fire recently?'

Keany made a quick double take. 'How did you hear that?'

'Been to a couple of your gigs,' I said. 'I kept hearing *Neddy* and *fire* in the same sentence.'

'He had a barbecue on his rooftop. We were there, but the drama happened after we left. I guess he didn't put the cinders out, but the neighbours managed to use that as grounds to kick him out of their building. Lucky bastards.'

'Now that *is* rock 'n' roll.'

Keany didn't look impressed.

'It's so weird buying a sandwich off you,' I said. 'What do the other guys in the band do?'

'Neddy starts fires, Jude has a pizza place in Dalston, Nathan's an electrician, he wired up this place.'

'Oh? I need a guy. Do you have his number?'

Keany's face crinkled at the strangeness of the sudden request, then he shrugged, got out his phone and read me off Nathan's phone number.

I texted the number, explaining a job I wanted doing. Nathan replied. We exchanged a couple of texts and he said he'd be at my place at 3pm.

Keany handed me my sandwich, braised beef, beetroot, salsa, other bitty things, and the crisps looked like they'd add a nice crunch.

I thanked him, took my tea and sarnie and paid with a generous tip. I browsed the library and noticed a Poirot mystery I'd probably read before, but I scanned the back cover and couldn't remember the plot or ending.

I plucked out the paperback and took a seat. The sandwich was surprisingly special, with bits of pomegranate, pickled grape and tarragon. The comforting carb helped the less than par state I was in. It was how I imagined sandwiches in America were like, that people talked about in movies in New York accents. London town — it seemed — was getting there, always twenty or so years behind.

Five cups of tea later, I'd read a third of the Poirot, and wasn't ready to place my money on who'd dunnit. I absentmindedly slipped the book into my back pocket, waved goodbye to Keany and jumped on the tube to get back to the flat to meet Nathan.

I had enough time for a quick shower before Nathan's arrival. He had a full but neat beard and a mass of dark hair on his head that, from a distance, could have been mistaken for a bicycle helmet.

I explained the hall light didn't work. 'I tried changing the bulb, and it's not the fuse.'

'When did it stop working?'

'I don't know. I've been here a year and it's not worked in that time.'

'And you never got it sorted?' he asked accusingly.

I wanted to retort, the girl upstairs had lived here longer than me, and she never did anything. Instead, I said, 'When people come round, I open my door at the top so they have some light to find their way up.'

'What about when *you* come up?'

'I tread carefully.'

Nathan unscrewed the light switch and pulled it away from the wall. 'The cables have just fallen away from the circuit.'

It took him five minutes to fix it. I handed him his fee. 'That should be the easiest fifty quid you make today.'

Nathan shrugged. 'You'd be surprised.' Something about these musicians, they weren't allowed to show any

The Highgate Murder

emotion. Maybe it all went into their music, except for Neddy's rage.

'I'm embarrassed at my ignorance,' I said. 'My dad used to do this work. He did everything himself. If he could see me now.'

'It happens a lot,' Nathan said sportingly. 'Ninety-nine percent of what I do for other people, their parents could have managed.'

'Good fall back job if rock stardom doesn't work out,' I said. 'I'm a fan of the band, by the way. I've bumped into Jude and Keany a few times.'

'Oh right.'

'Not spoken to Neddy though.'

I saw the muscles in Nathan's face tighten.

'Keany reckons you've got a chance to go far if it wasn't for your charismatic guitarist.'

'Yeah, maybe, but he won't leave us alone.'

'I heard. Why don't you all leave the band and start up again without him?'

'And do what? Play gigs? He'd be there. It's obvious we'd be the same band. Then there are all the songs we've written together. What are we supposed to do about them?'

'Yeah, those songs really are something,' I said. 'How have you managed this long?'

'When we're making music, he's focused, isn't that much of an arsehole. The rest of the time...' He trailed off. 'I personally stay as far away from him as I can. How the other guys cope, you'd have to ask them.'

'Sounds like you guys are trapped.'

'Completely trapped. I've got no idea what I'm supposed to do. Just as well I'm a qualified electrician.'

He looked very down and out.

'He's got a pretty girl. How does he manage that?'

'Some chicks like dicks.'

'I know that much.'

'I mean... bastards.'

'Oh right.'

'Before Jane, he was with another girl for a long time. She was gorgeous too. He utterly screwed her over. I think he ended up moving into her parents' house, threw a party while everyone was out and wrecked the place.'

'Set fire to it?' I asked.

'Nah. Just got drunk and smashed things up.'

'Is he on drugs?

'Nothing hard, that I know of.' He shrugged. 'Just a dick.'

Hatred was oozing off him, like Neddy had him over a barrel and he felt his musical career was going nowhere while this dickhead was on the scene.

'So, you won't start another band, but you might give up music altogether and spend your time doing this?' I was trying to sympathise with him, though I'd heard the music.

He surprised me and said, 'Things will sort themselves out.'

'How?'

'I don't know. They did for the Stones.'

'What do you mean?'

'Brian Jones drowned in a swimming pool, and Mick and Keith got control of the band, just like they wanted all along.'

'Right,' I said. 'Shame Neddy doesn't have a pool.'

'You're telling me.'

8

Nathan left. A couple of leads had popped up and I was feeling energised, this morning's despair a distant memory.

The band wanted Neddy out of their lives. That, on top of his winning personality, may have pushed someone to their limit. Nathan, I was confident, had the know-how. If Neddy got prison time, that could be the space the band needed to distance themselves from him and get a replacement musician. Knowing how to play guitar wasn't exactly a necessary requirement.

He'd also told me about a potentially bitter ex-girlfriend. A little social media stalking and I'd be able to rustle up her name.

I found Neddy on Facebook and scrolled through years of photos in ten seconds, backstage at gigs, scowling at the camera with pretty young people, usually with a drink in one hand and a cigarette in the other. His facial expression always seemed like it was saying 'Fuck you.'

A girl appeared beside him for a run of photos, a pale, pretty face with a ski-slope nose, made to seem paler by her dark brown eyes, painted lips and long dark hair. Poppy Ruiz. I clicked through to Poppy's profile to discover she was a self-employed T-shirt designer, along with her phone number.

The T-shirts were black or white, mostly plain, except for some branding on the trim of the sleeves. A few had small illustrations on the front, silhouettes of cut-out paper animals like an elephant or a swan. Each of them cost hundreds of pounds. Whether it was art collecting or fashion, how some things decided they were high end was a funny thing — not something I ever tried to get my mind around.

I figured the ex-girlfriend wouldn't be part of Neddy's current scene, so I planned to approach her with the truth about who I was. I didn't want to turn into one of those sleuths who got so used to lying they start doing it compulsively.

I called the number. After three rings, a throaty voice answered. 'Pie designs.'

'Is this Poppy?'

'Yes.'

'My name is Mike Seferis. I'm a detective investigating a potential case of arson involving one Neddy Mara.'

'Oh god. What did he do?'

'I'd like to explain that and ask you a few questions in person, hopefully today.'

'I was his girlfriend. Years ago. I don't understand what help I could be. I'm quite busy.'

'He doesn't have many close acquaintances. I'm trying to find anyone who can give me a sense of him. It won't take long and I'll come to wherever is convenient for you.'

'My office?'

'Sure.'

She gave me the address, in Covent Garden. I said I'd come straight over, jumped on the tube, and got there before five.

HER OFFICE WAS prime real estate. This young entrepreneur must have been shifting a lot of expensively branded T-shirts, or be independently wealthy. In the heart of bustling Covent Garden, I turned into a quiet side street of squat, brown-brick, terraced houses — housing for the poor in the days of Oliver Twist, now a row of pretty offices and holiday rentals.

I rang the bell, heard shuffling inside, and Poppy opened the door. Her hair was combed tall at the front, and into a ponytail. She wore a chunky, expensive-looking watch, two beaded bracelets and red nail varnish. Other than that, there was a simplicity to her look. She wasn't made up and didn't need to be. She wore a white T-shirt, a black blazer, tight black jeans with holes in the knees, and unfussy white plimsolls.

She looked me up and down. 'Detective Seferis?' she asked in her no-nonsense tone.

'In person.'

'Do you want to come in?'

'Sure.'

Her mature countenance contradicted her actions. I'd been vague about what kind of detective I was, and was ready to show my ID — a PI's licence — and go into further explanation. I also expected to have our conversation in her doorway.

She turned her back on me and led me through a hallway.

To the left, I could see through to a large bedroom where

a shower cubicle had been awkwardly installed at the foot of the bed, the owner of the property squeezing mod-cons into an old build as best they could.

So, this was her home-office, and it looked like she was alone. Maybe I had trustworthy eyebrows.

She led me into the main room, a large, open-plan living room and workspace, with a straight kitchen against the back wall. Transparent plastic containers were piled as high as they could go, full of coloured textiles. Her workstation was in the centre of the room; machines, frames, screens and buckets of paint surrounded her.

She sat on a purple sofa with corners and tucked her feet beneath her. I sat at the other end.

'So Neddy set something on fire,' she said, almost playfully.

I smiled despite myself. 'I didn't quite say that.'

She shrugged. 'I know.' She wasn't smiling, but I sensed she was amused by all this.

'He is being accused of setting fire to his building with intent to harm. I'm not sure if he did it. I thought if I went back far enough, I'd hear about another Neddy, before the rage.'

'You'll have to go back further than the time I knew him.'

'But you were together?'

'Yes,' she sighed. 'What can I say? I was young. I was stupid. I liked the music. I guess I liked the bad boy in him, but it got tiresome.'

'How long were you together?'

'Two years.'

'That's a long time.'

'A very long time, including a year he dossed with me and my folks.'

'You must have pretty patient folks.'

'You have no idea. I was fed up with Neddy a long time before they were. But it was wrong, putting my parents through that. He was awful. He took other women there when he had the place to himself, left used condoms in the sink.'

'Jesus.'

'I know, and he'd borrow money from them.'

'Do you know he comes from money?'

A convincing expression of surprise came over her face. 'If he does, he really enjoys slumming it.'

'Do you know anything about his family?'

'I didn't know he *had* a family.'

'Not a word about them in all that time?'

'If I ever asked him, he'd dismiss it. His face would twist like it was a distasteful subject, like he wasn't going to go there, like they weren't any good.'

'I can imagine a lot of wannabe rockstars are reluctant to admit they have parents, not to mention wealth.'

'I guess,' she said, shaking her head in disbelief.

'Was he ever physically abusive?'

She shook her head, but said, 'He slapped me in the face once, not hard, just a lazy *fuck you*.'

'Good for you for finally getting out of it.'

She reddened. '*He* got out of it. Guess he got bored. He moved out and got his own place, and I wasn't invited. Didn't actually *tell* me what was happening with us, but I got the message. And now I hear that's the tip of the iceberg of what he didn't tell me. He's sitting on a pile of money too.'

'Do you think he's capable of arson?'

She thought it over. 'I don't know. He lacks something. Feeling? Empathy? He likes to enjoy himself. He's not interested in you unless he thinks there's something you can do for him. It's a big leap from that to what he's been accused of doing.'

'Did he ever have a dog while you knew him?'

'What?'

'In the brief moment I was speaking to him, I saw him being abusive to a small dog. Again, I'm just trying to understand him. Twice he's chosen to live in quiet neighbourhoods mostly populated by mums who spend their time going to yoga and walking their cockerpoos. It doesn't suit him, and he doesn't seem to be enjoying it, but he's stubbornly digging his heels in, and he's even got himself a cute furry dog he seems to hate.'

'No, he never had a dog in the time I knew him. Maybe someone gave it to him, trying to domesticate him by giving him an animal to look after.'

'Hardly fair on the animal.'

She didn't look too happy with my comment. I wondered if the moment had come where I'd outstayed my welcome.

I was set to thank her and leave, but she said, 'You say he comes from money. Maybe he's a little prince whose whole image is actually an act of rebellion and he grew up in a pretty house with a teddy bear dog. And maybe a few drugs have affected his brain along the way.'

I nodded, a clever assessment. And she took it further by saying, 'You're not a police detective, are you?'

'I'm private. I've been hired by a relation of Neddy's to help him out.'

She nodded, expressionless. 'Would you like a drink? I'm having one myself.'

'No, thank you.'

She left the sofa and poured herself a glass of whisky on the other side of the room. I ran some closing sentences through my head — *thanks for your time, enjoy your drink.* They didn't seem appropriate now she was settling in.

She returned to the sofa, crossed her legs and leaned back, her arm along the back of the sofa.

'Do you think Neddy did it?'

'Too early to say. A clever device was set up in a calculating way. That's something I don't think he's capable of, but I still don't have a line on him. He can't be just all one thing.'

'Can't he? I have the feeling he's going to make it big. I know many people who've made it to the top of their field. The thing they all have in common is they're all arseholes.'

'I can't see him getting that far if his own band can't stand him, and if he manages to shout his way into a jail sentence.'

'Bad publicity is good publicity,' Poppy said.

'I hadn't thought of that angle.'

'I'm stupid for letting it go on for so long. I look back on it and think, what the hell was I doing? But I don't entirely regret what happened. I'd never let a man walk all over me again. Fear kept me in it. I didn't want to be on my own.'

She glanced at my hand, perhaps my wedding ring. 'Do you remember being on the dating scene?'

'Don't remind me.'

'I don't have a thing in common with a single guy out there. *I have this job, I have this much money, I have this many followers.* Where's the soul, you know?'

She talked me through a few amusing nightmare dates and made me chuckle, casually dangling her glass at an angle between her finger and thumb. I told her a few of Bill's funny stories that were fresh in my mind.

'How long have you been married?' she asked.

'Five years.'

'You were never tempted to screw around?'

'The thought never occurred to me.'

'You're one of the good ones. She's lucky.'

'You don't know me well enough to say that.'

I could see in her face she sensed something was amiss. 'Were you ever with the police?' she asked.

'For a while,' I said. 'It was something I always wanted to do. Things didn't go as I'd planned.' I noticed myself playing with the ring on my hand. 'Nothing went as I'd planned.'

'What happened?'

'I let her down.'

She didn't reply. The silence made me go on. 'I didn't protect her. There was a dark force in her life. I should have known. I should have worked it out sooner.'

'It's not your fault,' Poppy said. Her hand was on my thigh. I didn't know how long it had been there. I appreciated its warmth.

'You don't know that,' I said. I wondered at what point my questioning had lost its focus and she'd commandeered the conversation.

'You're not together anymore, are you?'

'No,' I said. 'Another man came between us.'

～

THE OTHER MAN was her brother, Paul. Alison had said little about him in the two years we'd been together. I got the impression he was an independent soul who'd neglected and forgotten about his family.

One night, we'd been at the pub and came home to find him waiting outside our house, strolling back and forth, hands in his pockets.

He shared Alison's handsome genes. His long face was

boyish and clean cut. His wavy, film-star hair had been combed neatly into place.

There didn't seem to be any love lost between them in the moment they embraced. He stayed in the spare room for a few days, and I could see things became strained between them. They seemed to be having some serious conversations when I was out of their hair, and I chose not to think anything of it.

He and I made an effort to be friendly, but we didn't click. If we tried to josh, the joke never landed. He tried to rib me for being a copper, and I tried to laugh it off, but there was more than just good-natured ribbing going on. He had an innate dislike for anyone who worked for 'the man' and would work himself up into a humourless righteousness. For my part, when he talked about coming back to London for a 'rest' after his exotic travels, I said something like, 'Sounds like you've had a rough time.' His grin evaporated into a cold stare. I saw behind the mask.

He left on a quiet, non-celebratory note. Alison was tearful. It took her a couple of days to finally reveal Paul was a gambler. He said he'd gone to some dark places to borrow and now he needed money badly. She'd given him all her savings.

We'd had some money saved, each of us in our own accounts, hoping to get a mortgage on a home. Pap was keen for us to stop paying rent 'like mugs' and wanted to help us financially. Paul had come along and popped that balloon.

He returned a couple of years later. We were in the same flat in Stroud Green. He stayed in the spare room and we had a couple of awkward dinners. Then, abruptly, he was gone.

Alison panicked and told me what he'd told her. He'd needed some serious cash, six figures. He'd borrowed from dangerous men. When he failed to pay his debt, they'd beaten him and broken his jaw. When he missed the next deadline, they took him to a wood and made him dig his own grave. He pleaded with them and somehow got another chance.

So, he'd come to ask Alison, was there anyone she knew or any way she could help get the money together? By the time she'd recovered from the shock from what he'd told her and was ready to think things over properly, he'd left without a word.

She was frantic, but he called her a few days later and told her he'd got the money and was fine. He was vague about how he'd managed it. I was wary from that point onwards. I knew this thing was going to come back for us, but I didn't know what I was going to do about it.

So, I'd failed her. Because my instincts were right. The third time was the killer.

9

'Another man came between us,' I'd said vaguely. Poppy didn't pry further. She said, 'I'm going to have another drink. Will you join me this time?'

'Sure,' I said. I'd started to get jealous of the one she was holding. Goodness, how could that be, after a day hung so painfully far over? I guess the rich comfort and tingling amusement it promised.

It came in a rock glass with a thick, heavy base. A generous measure, the rounded, peaty taste was a relief after the alcoholic spirit from yesterday. She brought the bottle with her and sat closer to me.

'Cheers.' She raised her glass.

We asked about each other's work and kept things light while my mind replayed the past, the what ifs, the could haves, the should haves. Poppy topped our glasses up along the way. Then she took my drink out of my hand, placed it on the table, and came closer. I felt her lips, her hands, neither of which were entirely unpleasant.

She took me to bed and put me to work. The exertion and booze sent me to sleep shortly thereafter. But not for long. She must have jumped out of bed and got dressed. 'Mike!'

I sat up and shook my head to orientate myself. 'Yes?'

'I'm going out. I need you to leave.' She wore a smirk of distaste, like this had been an elaborate joke, or I was an elaborate joke. Her head was turned to the side so she didn't have to look directly at me.

I massaged my face, got out of the bed and dressed. It was humiliating. I'd never be able to describe the perfect nuance of her actions, but she knew exactly what she was doing. It was like a professional hit. If one gesture was a second longer or shorter, her unspoken dislike for me wouldn't have translated as well. Everything was so perfectly executed to make me feel like shit.

'Are you okay?' I asked.

'Sure,' she said with awkward inflection, as if waiting for an embarrassing moment to pass, hopefully as quickly as possible.

'I'll let myself out then,' I said. I left the apartment without saying another word or looking back.

I crossed over Drury Lane and had a quick beer at The Cross Keys to ground myself. What the hell had just happened? A stranger had seduced me and cut me down. I couldn't believe I'd told her about Alison. It made the whole ordeal more sordid. And all because she'd had a pretty face. Why do men forget everything when a pretty face smiles at them?

Maybe she was getting her own back on men. She sounded vengeful. Could sleeping with a wounded man, then laughing at him and throwing him out be a hint of what she was capable of? Could she afford to pay someone to set up a fire-starting device to cause Neddy trouble? She'd stuck it out for two years, then she'd been dropped without even being informed. That was motive. But that was going on what she'd told me. How was I supposed to believe any of it? She'd been playing with me from the moment she'd invited me over.

But what did it matter? I had to go to work. In that moment, I felt that work was the answer, the only answer to indignity, loss, mortality. Riding in Pap's car, he once talked about the satisfying nature of his work. His wife had left him to raise me on his own, and other aspects of life had knocked him about; but the unshakable focus of his jobs, looking after his properties and the people in them, was everything.

He ran his business in a way that helped people. I wanted to be a copper to help people. My present job wasn't that kind of work. From the moment I tried to solve the Incident to this current fiasco — living the dream, as Bill put it — I wasn't doing any good for anyone. I was just amusing myself. I thought I'd allow myself that indulgence after Alison died. What else was there?

The memory of Pap's words helped me shake off the events of the last hour and set off for my next appointment. I had to get a taxi to get me back to north London in a timely fashion.

Winners was near Arsenal's old stadium. Gunners posters adorned the walls behind the counter. It was a no-nonsense kebab shop, with the rotating slab of donor in the window and hungry masses chowing down on good quality babs on plastic tables and chairs. It was also an institution, had been around longer than any of the kids in there, chowing their babs, and had gradually become a hub for young people to sit around in, drinking bottled beer.

It also contained a third, almost clandestine identity. I told the man behind the counter I was here to see Steve in the back. He nodded, and I went through to the back restaurant. Pap brought me here only a couple of times and I remembered my surprise when we walked through what seemed like a secret doorway into another world. The air was thick with smoke. Greek-Cypriot men congregated, ranging from middle-aged to old, drinking Greek coffee and eating delicacies off small plates.

Steve Korona, real name Stefanos Koronos (it paid to anglicise your name and assimilate back in the day), had been around a lot when I was a kid growing up in West Finchley. Like an uncle, I remember regularly getting birthday cards from him with a fiver inside. Pap and I would visit his big happy family, and they would visit us in Finchley and sit in our garden eating watermelon on summer days.

His sons were older than me and they'd knock me about a bit. I get them mixed up with kids of Pap's other friends as, somehow, they were all older and bigger, and all knocked me about a bit. I had a dozen names and faces in my mind that might have belonged to Steve's two sons.

I saw him sitting at a corner table reading a paper, holding a cigarette and coffee cup in the same hand. He had a big, round nose that matched his swollen, Father-Christmas cheeks — accentuated by his big grin. He had a white, neatly trimmed beard and immaculately neat grey hair in a side parting. He wore a black jumper with the collar of a black shirt poking out.

He looked up and shot up with an immediacy that would have made me light-headed, and I was half his age.

'Mike!' his warm, heavy voice boomed as he pumped my hand in a death grip. 'How you doing, son?'

'Alright, Steve. You're looking well.'

Steve laughed and called to a waiter for a bottle of

zivania and two glasses. Oh shit, I thought.

A young, mustachioed waiter appeared with a bottle of Cypriot grappa and poured two tumblers halfway. He eyed Steve's paper as he poured. 'Any good tips?'

Steve laughed. He'd been looking at the horses. 'No,' he said. 'Just checking the form. Force of habit.' He gestured at me. 'This is Mike, Nikos's son.'

The waiter looked disinterested, but said, 'This is on the house.' This struck me as a very Greek-Cypriot gesture. Half the time, in the Greek-Cypriot grocers in Crouch End, they eye me and ask if I'm Greek-Cypriot. I tell them I am. They tell me my bread and coffee are on the house. Same as with the waiter, they're not particularly friendly, and they're not reluctant, it's just no-nonsense solidarity. I had to wonder, if a Greek-Cypriot came to my office with a job, should they get a discount?

I thanked the waiter and said to Steve. 'I haven't been here since I was a kid.'

'It's a good place to pass the day,' Steve said. 'After Linda died, this place became a haven for me, familiar faces, have a coffee and a game of chess.' He had a constant grin and spoke in a world-weary, amused tone, like nothing bothered him too much.

'Sounds like being in the old country,' I said.

'Without the sunshine.'

We drank. He said, 'I was sorry to hear about your wife.'

'Thanks.'

'Your pap was crazy about her. What was her name?'

'Alison.'

'Alison. Couldn't have been happier you married a musician, unless maybe if you'd have become one yourself. Didn't he introduce you both or something?'

'Not exactly, I was just accompanying him on one of his

jazz pilgrimages.'

Steve laughed. 'That was a relief. Before you were old enough, he used to drag me along to those things.'

I laughed along. 'Tiny gig in a basement in Soho, less than a dozen people. Alison sits down and says, *Hello, Wembley!*'

Steve laughed louder, a nostalgic sound I liked, taking me back to sunny days of yore.

'Criminal,' I went on. 'The amount of people uninterested in actual musicians these days.'

'That's what I was trying to tell your pap years ago.' Steve said. '*You* may like it, but people don't go to bars to drink martinis and listen to jazz piano like they're in a Billy Wilder film. He always wanted to run a little Soho piano bar, like he was living in the fifties or something. He set it up and hired a piano player, a French guy. For months, no one showed. I told him, people want to drink and talk. Finally, he took my advice, sold the piano, bought a jukebox, and he made a success of it. And the next best thing happened. Musicians from Ronnie Scott's would go there for a drink after hours. We met Nina Simone there.'

I knew all this, maybe not this version of it, but I nodded along.

'Soho was a lot different in those days, gangsters, pimps, prostitutes. But they seem like the good old days now. Gentrification and *Airbnbs* popping up everywhere, Soho's going to lose the essence of why people go there in the first place. Hard to imagine your mild-mannered old man at the centre of it all, but he was fearless.'

He topped up our glasses. The zivania almost tasted like smooth, sweet schnapps to me after the Dublin Castle's 'alcohol spirit'. It took immediate effect. Steve's chatting, laughing face was swimming in front of me like a dream.

'I don't know if he ever told you, when these *Italians* came into La Roca, they brought a cigarette machine with them. "We'll be back at the end of the day to collect the takings," they said. They weren't talking about profits from the machine.'

I shook my head. I hadn't heard this one.

'I didn't say a thing. I think I was in shock. Your pap didn't say anything either. He kept himself busy for twenty minutes; I guess, thinking things over. Then, as casual as anything, he said, "Help me push this thing outside." We pushed it outside and I spent the rest of the afternoon with him. He didn't say another word about it. They returned before the day was over and he told them, "I didn't order anything from you and I'm not doing business with you." They stared him down. He didn't blink. And he got away with it. Never heard from them again.'

'I never knew he could be so gutsy,' I said.

'The ironic thing about that is, your pap never made any money because he was so big-hearted — he was always giving it away. But someone leaned on him and he wouldn't give an inch.'

Steve was there, in the past, with his old friend. The present caught up with him and I saw him wince at a stab of pain. 'He deserved better luck.'

He went back to the beginning, friends as kids — neighbours in Archway, going to Arsenal matches together. They'd often see their idols in *Winners* after games, back when footballers lived on kebabs and beer, before it was a multimillion-pound industry.

He told a story about going to an Arsenal game from my own memory bank, not remembering the three of us had been together that day. (His own boys had chosen to follow local rivals, Spurs, so he was stuck with us.) 'One time, they were playing Leeds, back when tickets cost a tenner. The game was about to start and we didn't have tickets yet. It was my turn to pay. We found a tout, and he said, 'Thirty quid for two tickets.' I said, 'Twenty,' and he wasn't having it. Sounds crazy now, but I stood firm. We haggled, and I walked away. He called after me, 'You win!' and gave me the tickets for twenty. Turned out, your pap had slipped him the extra tenner behind my back!'

It wasn't Leeds but a Villa game. The tout wanted forty quid for three tickets. I saw the whole thing, Pap subtly slipping the guy the extra tenner, winking at me with that big grin of his. I remember thinking this was the coolest guy in the world. Magnum PI had nothing on him.

'His generosity drove your mother crazy. He bought that property in Wembley. A sweet old lady lived there, so he never upped her rent, and spent all his time and money doing the place up for her.

'Meanwhile, we had that big house and the swimming pool. I think your mother resented that. But look how that turned out.'

Steve had had gambling issues, which put a strain on the family. He'd separated from his wife before she'd died and wasn't on good terms with his boys last I'd heard.

'Sad irony was, he wanted to be a family man. Gave up the club, he said, because he wanted to be a pap who left for work in the mornings, and arrived home at the same time every evening.

'It bothered her. What happened to the drive he had that had made him so successful? And she left. I don't know if you knew that version of the story. Knowing Nick, he probably painted her in a more sympathetic light.'

'I contacted her a couple of times and got the cold shoulder,' I said. 'That told me all I need to know.'

I could see the zivania taking effect in his eyes. 'And you lost Nick and your wife at the same time. I wouldn't wish that on anyone. How much did he know about what was going on?'

'He was very sick when she died. I couldn't tell him the violent truth. I told him she'd been in an accident. He was crushed but...' I trailed off.

'Yeah,' Steve nodded. 'The truth would have been hard to handle. And what you did next. He wouldn't have been thrilled about that either.'

As invincible as the booze made me feel, I lowered my eyes away from his stare.

'They taught you all that in the police force?' he prodded.

A couple of retorts popped into my head, but I didn't engage.

'And now you're asking about Derek O'Mara,' he said. 'Are you looking to get into real estate and smashing knee caps?'

'It's for my work,' I said.

Steve looked pensive, like he was thinking up the right words or approach. 'Michael, what's done is done.'

'I know.'

'So why are you still looking for trouble? Your old man never did.'

'I'm not my old man.'

'In some ways you are, but because you can't be him, be liked by everyone, you go the other way, stirring up all kinds of shit. Is this thing worth it?'

'It's my work. It's what I do.'

'As stubborn as your old man.'

I shrugged.

'How has Derek got onto the radar of the great detective, then?'

'Something to do with his family,' I said.

Steve let out a slow breath and shook his head, stunned at the audacity. 'Mike, I don't think he'd appreciate you nosing in on his private life.'

'I know that much. What else can you tell me?'

Steve sighed. 'He's got a lot of Soho properties. He's not allowed to, but he rents them out on short lets. And he's got a bar on Wardour street, Dutch Pink.'

'I know it,' I said. I'd walked by it enough times.

'I don't know what else I can tell you.'

'You could tell me you're going to give him a call and say I want to talk to him.'

He searched my eyes. I wondered what he was looking for. 'Did you try bereavement counselling?'

Our relationship had never gone beyond avuncular and jovial. This new, serious tone felt awkward, like a parent sitting you down for your first talk about the birds and the bees.

'The Met assigned me to a couple of counsellors. Before I spoke, they started prescribing pills. *You need anti-depressants, you need sleeping pills...* I could have cut out the middle man and taken my issues straight to the pharmacist. I didn't pursue it. I was irritated by the theory that the answer could be found in a substance.'

'Counsellors don't prescribe drugs,' Steve said. 'Only GPs and psychiatrists do that.'

'What would you know?'

'I've been bereaved and I've had bereavement counselling.' He pulled an ancient Nokia phone out of his pocket and placed it on the table. 'I got support quitting gambling too.'

At first, I didn't understand his gesture, then it came to me that having a smart phone and the internet in your pocket is a bit like carrying around a 24/7 casino.

'Okay,' I said, rolling my eyes at having to expand on my pithy version of events. 'They didn't directly prescribe pills. They said they wanted to work with my GP on that. I wasn't resisting support.'

His expression was disbelieving. 'Counsellors believe in the talking cure, not pills.'

'That wasn't the experience I had.'

'Then maybe you need to look further into it and deal with what happened, instead of charging around Soho, knocking heads together, in the hope it'll get you killed. After what happened with your wife, the likes of me and every person your father knew had to vouch for you, saying you had nothing to do with what happened. You've played that card now. When is this going to end?'

'When I say it does.'

Steve rolled his eyes and sat back in his chair. We had a stare off. Finally, he picked up his phone and focused his glazed eyes on its screen.

He made the call. 'Derek? This is Steve Korona. I'm having a drink with Mike Seferis, Nick's son. Nick the Greek. He wants to meet you and asked me for an introduction. He didn't say what it's about.'

He listened for a moment before looking at the phone, surprised by the abrupt end of the call.

'He's at the club now if you want to go over,' he said. 'You better go right now before I change my mind.'

'Thanks, Steve,' I said. 'I'll be fine.'

Steve picked up his glass, saw it was empty. The wry grin and carefree armour had returned. 'Sure you will.'

10

It was drizzly and dark when I stumbled out of *Winners* and cabbed back south, feeling like a yo-yo being tossed down and up between north and central London.

I sank into the back seat like a deflated tyre, watching the cabbie's headrest spin. As we approached Soho, I got out for a sobering walk through the maze of tiny streets, full of noise, lights, hip joints and history.

I felt so unsteady, I focused on the people, rambunctious, almost desperate in their need to consume booze as quickly as they could.

I had a flashback to Soho's 'good old days', as Steve called them. A sketchy red-light district, all of today's tapas and sushi restaurants were strip clubs and adult video stores, with boarded-up windows and ribbon-feted doorways.

A curious kid — what kid wouldn't be? — I tried to drink it all in from the corner of my eye, trying to seem disinterested in the colourful depravity, while being led about by my pap to another jazz hole.

The Highgate Murder

. . .

BUT THAT WAS THEN and this was now. I had a very different kind of evening ahead, with a very different kind of character. There was a line outside of Derek's place. I made my way to an open doorway round the side and said to the man standing there, 'Mike Seferis to see Derek.'

He asked if I had an appointment. I said I did.

'Go on then,' he said, nodding at the darkness.

Up a dark stairway was another club in itself, red lighting, eerily empty. Throbbing drum and bass from downstairs made the floor vibrate; an open area in the centre for dancing or milling, if people were ever here to dance or mill; a couple of small tables with chairs; a bar at the far end, with two heavy set men on either side of it, one to serve the drinks, the hulkier one sitting on a stool. Both had their eyes on me.

I turned to my right to see a nook with mirrored walls and cushioned seats surrounding a low table. There sat Derek O'Mara. I'd heard about him, but it was still a surprise to behold. In this showy club, full of showy people, sat a bald, big-bellied man in his mid-sixties, with a beard of bristly white stubble, in a stained T-shirt.

'Looks like a hobo, but he's a nutter,' was a common phrase I'd heard bandied about.

To his right was a younger man with reddish hair gelled back over his head, and a bulge in his suit jacket.

'This must be Mike, son of Nick the Greek,' Derek said in a gravelly voice.

'And you must be Derek, father of Neddy Mara.'

Anyone's advice would have been to choose my words with the utmost care. I hadn't. I saw the expression of lazy disinterest leave his face and his chest heave as he pulled in a lungful of air. The hairs on the back of my neck prickled. He turned to his man and made the slightest of nods. His man sidled out of his seat and approached.

He stopped a yard away from me. His hand went into his jacket. I shifted my feet. When the gun appeared, I kneed him in the stomach and made a clumsy grab for the gun. It was basic police training, or something like it, but I didn't fancy my chances — you mess around with Derek O'Mara's bodyguard, you're leaving in a body bag.

The gun came away in my hand. Derek's man was bent over, winded, trying to pull himself up again. Adrenaline was surging within me. I was expecting the two other men to rush me.

Derek's man straightened, eyes blazing with anger. We were at a standoff. I held the gun by the barrel and gestured the weapon back to him.

Derek started laughing his head off. 'He's an Argo-nut!'

His man looked at me and looked at the gun. Maybe I was giving away my last chance to get out of there. Derek's roaring laughter was making it hard for anyone to think.

Finally, Derek had to instruct him. 'Ricky, take your gun and put it away. Shane, get him a drink. What do you want, kid?'

I couldn't think of an answer. What did I want? Why did I come here? Not to be offered a drink. I had to search my mind to even think of what I could say. 'Er... whisky,' I said. Yes, that was a drink.

He nodded to a chair. 'Take a seat.' I took it just in time. I was shaking so badly I could hardly stand.

Derek was eyeing me. I returned his stare. A drink appeared on the low table before me. Without breaking eye contact, he said, 'Why don't you give us a moment alone, lads?'

'Boss—' Ricky protested in a heavy Irish drawl.

'Go have a drink downstairs,' Derek said.

People left the room. Derek had to say, 'You too, Shane,' to get rid of them all.

We shared a silence. He nodded at my whisky and told me to have a drink. I did.

'I've heard of you, boy,' he said. 'But I wasn't expecting that. There must have been a hard wind when you fell from the tree.'

I was looking away from him, feeling small and fearful. I felt like I'd gone three rounds bluffing big on a poker hand, acting like a big man. Now I wanted to back down and drop out of the game, but I summoned the will to look him in the eye again.

'Did you genuinely want to get your brains blown out all over my floor?'

'I don't know,' I croaked, my voice hoarse, not my own.

'Ricky's my nephew. I'm trying to keep him in work and out of trouble.'

'I see.'

'On another day...' He let his words hang in the air.

'I know.'

He took his time looking me over, trying to work me out, maybe. 'You lost your wife. I guess you don't care if you got lost too.'

Again, I found myself looking at my hands. I raised my eyes back to Derek.

'No one's a hundred percent sure about what you did to Harry Flett,' he said. 'The story, as far as I know, is Harry ordered a hit on someone who crossed him, and Compston, Harry's trigger-happy minder, shot and killed the target's sister. That sister was the wife of a young Argo-nut copper, who went on a rampage through Soho, asking a lot of questions and stepping on a lot of toes. He's wet behind the ears and no one takes him very seriously. Then Compston is shot dead, and all Harry's dodgy dealings catch up with him and he ends up doing life. Could the young Argo-nut have anything to do with all that spilt blood?'

'My wife got caught in the crossfire of something and I was determined to find some answers. Then a lot of gangsters start shooting at each other — that's got nothing to do with me.'

'So you say,' said Derek, looking very unconvinced, and... slightly amused? 'If I gave a toss about those goons...' He let the words hang in the air. I held his gaze.

'What's Neddy done to get the great Argo-nut detective on his case?'

'Arson,' I said, pleased for the abrupt shift in conversation. 'Someone set fire to his apartment. It's possible he even did it himself.'

'Sounds like Neddy. Who's paying you?'

A thought crossed my mind about client confidentiality. It was brief and fleeting. 'Edward Donsaw.'

Derek's dark eyes became tiny dots. I could feel the hairs on my neck again. I waited him out. Finally, he said, 'What are you? Some VIP shamus to the upper class?'

'No... I... he called me up and asked me to look into a matter. I didn't know who Neddy was at that point.'

'But you know who Donsaw is?'

'I didn't at the time. I've looked into him since, some blue blood.'

'How did he know about you?'

'*You* know about me.'

'He and I don't exactly run in the same circles.'

'He just said he'd heard about me. What are you getting at?'

The Highgate Murder

'I'm wondering if you knew how dangerous he is.'

'More than you?'

'More than *you*,' he said. 'It's different worlds, him and us. He's got money, power, he won't be crossed.'

'Guess I got suckered by his elegant manners,' I said, almost amused to hear a fox talk about an elderly rabbit this way.

He took a deep drink and sighed. I took a drink too, savouring the pleasant burn of aged Scotch. I managed not to sigh.

'Did Donsaw tell you why he's interested in Neddy?' Derek asked.

'He said he was a friend of the family.'

Derek scoffed. He sipped his drink, smacked his lips and said softly, 'A friend of the family.' He seemed to mull it over as he leaned forward to roll himself a cigarette from a pouch of tobacco on the table. Without looking up, he asked, 'Have you met Neddy?'

'Yeah.'

'Do you see a family resemblance?'

'What do you mean?'

'You know I'm not the father?'

'Uh huh,' I mumbled noncommittally.

'Neddy's mum, Catherine; I had a soft spot for her, used to watch her on TV. She started coming to my club, same in person as on the telly, bright and cheeky like a peach in summer. Then she went off with those upper-class types, saw what they were really made of, and came back here and threw her lot in with me, a shady club owner. She wanted nothing to do with that family after the view into their world she had. It had traumatised her. She wasn't my giggling young Barbara Windsor anymore, didn't like to go out and have fun, and eventually got scared of just going out. She came to me because she knew I'd protect her.'

'Protect her from what?'

'She could never tell me. But she was terrified of that family. She told me she was having a kid. The father was one of the sons of his royal highness, Edward Donsaw. I said I'd be a father to the kid, that's what it says on the official documents. I tried to be. He was an utter bastard from the moment he could talk. From the age of three he was like a difficult teenager, and when he hit his teens, he was off the grid.'

Derek leaned back and lit his roll-up. I couldn't believe this open, personal dialogue we were having. He talked in a calm, almost gentle manner, like this was a bedtime story. This was the legendary Derek O'Mara that coppers were wary of, that Steve had been reluctant to introduce me to? I'd stormed in like a bull. Derek had taken the bait, then cracked up laughing, and was now telling me his family history over whisky and cigarettes. Should I have been worried? Was this a menacing, misleading softness? Was this the villain getting everything off his chest before feeding his foe to the fishes? Or did he see me as a kindred nutjob — after taking Ricky's gun off him, then handing it back to him?

'We thought the Donsaws were history as far as we were concerned,' Derek went on. 'Then the patriarch reappeared and poked his claw in. When Neddy was in his mid-teens, Donsaw made contact and started bank rolling him. It took me a couple of years to realise Neddy was more flush than he should have been. I had it looked into. He didn't seem to be dealing drugs. So, I had some connections of mine check his bank records and I discovered the source. A steady, abundant income from his true grandfather.

'I kept my new found knowledge to myself. I didn't confront Neddy, and I didn't want to burden Catherine that the family she feared so much was interfering in our lives.

'I don't know what he whispered in his ear, but the bottom line is, he got to Neddy through money. Having all that money meant there was no way to discipline him. It was no teenage phase. He hated us, wore his mother down. Sometimes, he'd disappear and sever contact with us. It felt like a relief. But being a mother, Catherine would always start to miss him.

'A year ago, she was itchy to see him. He relented and she made arrangements. I didn't get involved. God knows what he said to her. I came home.' He took a deep inhale of his cigarette. 'She'd hung herself. I haven't seen him since and I don't talk about him. When little Greek boys barge into my place, bandying his name, I become an inhospitable host.'

I thought of saying sorry. My intention hadn't been to scratch a man's wound. But I was wary an apology could be seen as a sign of weakness, or sanity. He seemed to like me well enough so why change my act? 'Don't you... want to know what he said to her?' I asked.

'There was no magic bullet that made her do it. He wore her down for years, always knew what buttons to press, never missed an opportunity to hurt her. The boy was a bad seed, and Donsaw knew money would make it worse.'

I wondered if Derek had set the device to put an end to Neddy. Some would see it as justifiable, an eye for an eye. But I didn't ask the question.

He looked at his drink for a long time. I sipped at mine. We eventually finished them. He said, 'I'll have another drink. Fetch that bottle of MacGregor from behind the bar.'

I did his bidding. He filled our glasses. I suppose I'd

ingratiated myself. He liked to talk. He talked about how he liked to make money, something about how the banks approached him, eager to help him with his lucrative lettings endeavour. After Catherine's death, he preferred to be in Soho, with his finger on the pulse and his eye on the latest fashion and trends. What better way to do that than to run a nightclub? He told me where I could get cheap fry ups in the neighbourhood. He even went into his theories about how music and creative ideas were communicated to people by aliens. I think. I was pretty wasted by then.

11

One of his men checked in on us and Derek told him to put me in a taxi. I stumbled as I stood and staggered out of there, which Derek and his man found amusing. I had to stop the taxi before too long to get out and throw up in the street.

After that, I guess I hailed another cab to go home, paid the driver, got inside the flat, turned the lights and some music on, and fell asleep on the sofa bed without going to the trouble of transforming it into a bed; because I awoke by the dawn's early light, disorientated, house lights on, music blaring, and still alive.

I lay there staring at the ceiling. Memories from the previous night slowly filtered through to me.

If that bodyguard had been doing his job, all this would be over. I couldn't get my mind around how close it really came, and the idea didn't scare me as much as I'd hoped it would. I didn't have a sense of guilt for leaving anyone in any pain — except for the people who'd have to clean up the mess, but one day I'd be a mess for someone to clean up anyway.

No Alison, no parents.

There *was* Kim.

What did that mean? Someone on this earth, I believed, who would be truly saddened, affected, if I'd have done myself in? The thought did send a warmth through me. Should I call her and tell her I needed someone, needed help? I couldn't go on the way I had been anymore.

As if something cosmic was at play, the phone rang. I hoped it was her. I pulled myself off the sofa and got to the table where my phone lay. Her name was on the screen. I'd known it was her and was surprised as hell at the same time.

I said a croaky, 'Hey,' into the receiver.

'Hey, punk. You ready for tonight?'

I searched my brain for what she could mean. The thought that I might have an appointment that night and might have to do anything was petrifying. 'Eh?'

'Poker.'

It took a while, but I finally comprehended what she meant, and I wasn't happy about it. There was no way I could do a social that night. But I was even less able to turn Kim down. I said, 'I guess I can put in a quick appearance and give you guys my money.'

'You're going to have to do better than that. We're coming to your place. We want to see your Highgate pad and we're not taking *no* for an answer.'

I looked around the place, thinking the idea impossible. I'd never entertained there before, outside of having clients come directly into the office.

'I don't know,' was all I could say. I didn't have the fight in me.

'Well, I do. We're getting there at eight and we'll bring everything, booze, nibbles...'

'You might need to bring a deck of cards too,' I said.

'And the poker chips. I'm on it. It's going to be... very... interesting.'

'What does that mean?'

I could hear the smile in her cotton-soft voice. 'Oh, you'll see.'

She rang off. The idea was insane. Well, no. I'd been acting insane, and this was the sanest moment of the past twenty-four hours. I felt so numb, like my brain couldn't process the past day and was on a sabbatical.

I had nothing else pressing, couldn't think about the case. I put one foot in front of the other and did a minimal amount of tidying.

I WALKED to the cornershop a few doors down the road and bought two crates of near beer. I couldn't let myself touch the more potent stuff, but as the last few days showed, I was a sucker for peer pressure. With two crates of non-alcoholic beer, I'd feel obliged to drink the stuff or have it clog up twenty percent of the floor space of my kitchen.

I had a shower and fell into a dreamless sleep on the sofa with a towel around my waist for the rest of the day.

I awoke with minutes to spare. Dazed from the epic, all-day nap, I lay still for a while, then threw some clothes on as the buzzer went.

The gang had arrived all at once. I guess they wanted to see my reaction to what they had in store for me.

I opened the door and a dog, a little black fur ball, flew through the doorway and raced around the flat. I worried about him knocking things over like the electric heater, but he had an uncanny control. Though wriggling with excitement, he had the ability to go near a precarious object yet practice some kind of instinct not to knock it over. He squeezed himself into every nook and cranny to investigate every inch of the apartment. Some crannies were too tight for him to turn around and get out, so he'd wriggle backwards to free himself.

In the time it took for him to explore every inch of the place, Kim came in smiling. She was a skinny creature with a striking face, big green eyes, big lips and prominent cheekbones. She had hair the colour of chestnuts, and she pulled off a different hair style almost every time I saw her. Today, she had a becoming bob, tied up with a red bandanna.

The sight of her distracted me from the drama at hand. For a moment. The ecstatic dog wagged his tail so hard his entire body was a wriggling dance. He looked uncannily like the one I'd seen being abused by Neddy.

'Whose dog is that?' I asked.

'He doesn't have an owner right now,' Kim said. The gang, behind her, exchanged a variety of smiles and awkward glances.

'That isn't...?' I left the question hanging.

'The pup that once belonged to the lowlife you're investigating?' Kim said. 'Yes, it is.'

'What?'

'I contrived a reason to pay him a visit. I wasn't there for two minutes before he started abusing the dog in front of me. I said it wasn't on, and I confiscated the dog.'

'You can't do that.'

'You can if you happen to have someone from the RSPCA with you.'

'Okay,' I said. 'But... I don't understand why you brought him here.'

'You save an animal, you're responsible for it,' Kim said.

'But *you're* the one who saved it.'

'No, you did, when you reported it to the police.'

'That was conversational.'

'All talk is conversational.'

Bill, entering the abode and handing me his coat, said, 'You've done a good deed, saving him from an abusive owner and taking him in.'

'Guys, you can't just give me a dog. I'm not a dog person.'

'What's done is done,' Kim said. 'We can't give it back to someone we've reported as an abusive owner.'

'Dogs aren't like bottles of wine; you don't bring them to someone's house when you come around for dinner.'

'It's not dinner,' Kim said. 'It's a poker game.'

'Or a poker game.'

'And it's not from *me*. We all thought it was a good idea.'

'Well—' Bill began.

'Shut up, Bill,' Kim said.

'He's, like, your sidekick. The Wee Jock to your Hamish Macbeth,' Rellers said, adding her coat to the pile forming on my arm. Rellers worked in the Met in a trainer and lecturer capacity. She'd acquired her nickname, a shortened version of Cinderella, because she'd always be the first to leave the pub back in the day. *Hamish Macbeth*, for those not in the know, was a detective series set in the Scottish Highlands. Wee Jock was his loyal westie.

'Hamish Macbeth lives in Lochdubh, I live in London. And he's not real.'

'How dare you,' Rellers said.

'You heard me.'

'So you're not going to call him Wee Jock?'

'He has a name,' I said.

'No, he doesn't,' Kim said. 'All he got from his arsehole former owner was abuse. We didn't pause to ask him what he called his former pet aside from *punching bag*.'

'Kim, this is crazy.'

'Look at him!' Kim demanded.

Now it had explored the flat, it was shuffling around the room, doing his wriggle dance. And it was a *he*, apparently.

'He looks happy to be here,' Bill said.

I thought of all the people I knew who'd had dogs, how their houses smelled of dog, wet hair, mud and farts. In this tiny place, the smell would attach itself to me. 'I don't know about this.'

The dog continued to dance around the place like a pinball.

'He's not going anywhere for the time being,' Kim said. 'Let's play some cards and get into this later on.'

THE REST of the gang were in the flat now. They'd shaken my hand or punched my arm while I'd been distracted by the dog. They'd brought dog necessities: food, toys, poo bags and a soft dog bed — or a cushion basket — whatever you call them. They'd also brought everything required for a poker night.

Kim and I were the only ones still standing. The others had made themselves comfortable around the table. They'd put their beers in the fridge, and were munching nibbles they'd brought, catching up with each other, and piling poker chips.

'Beer?' Kim asked me.

'There's near beer in the fridge. I'll have one of those.'

Kim flinched, recovered, and said, 'Right.' I guess she didn't want to question me so soon after trying to push a pet onto me. She fetched me a near beer and set out a water bowl for the dog. The near beer tasted mostly good; refreshing, savoury, though with an acrid aftertaste.

We joined the collective. Bill sat to my right. He had

been cajoled into telling another story of failed romance. 'This one you won't believe,' he said. 'As cold as the Beast from the East; after a date, she wouldn't reply to my texts. So, I sent a final one, saying I was getting the message, she wasn't interested and I wished her the best. She messaged me back, saying on the contrary, would I like to take her to the movies?'

'But why were you even still interested if she wasn't nice?' Rellers asked.

Bill cast his eyes downward. 'She... wasn't... bad looking.'

The women of the group groaned. The men shifted awkwardly. The dog sniffed at the bookcase. I grimaced at the thought he might be about to mark his territory on it.

'She acted the same way on the second date,' Bill said. 'Cold as a Nordic noir. And I sent her a similar message. *I'm guessing you're not interested.* She said, let's meet up again and see another movie. Utter trite too. Anything with Leonardo DiCaprio. I mentioned a Pawel Pawlikowski retrospective at the BFI. She wasn't interested.'

'That's surprising,' Kim said.

'Anyway,' Bill said. 'Five films down the line, I don't know what's going on. Every time I ask for some clarification, she'd just suggest another film. I mean, what did she want from me? I finally leaned in for a kiss. She looked at me like I was a new car with a flat tyre. She backed off, ran away and that was last I saw of her.'

'Same thing happened to me!' said Patchy, my old flat-mate, a cheerful, chatty Intelligence Analyst, who laughed hysterically at all jokes and stories, including his own. 'Years ago,' he said. 'I dated a woman. She didn't seem interested in me at all but kept suggesting these dates to the cinema. When I finally suggested we do something else, she chucked me. I felt so used. I thought, women, they're only after one thing.'

'A cinema companion?' Kim clarified.

'Right!'

'Maybe it was the same woman,' I said. I got one laugh and a lot of groans.

'Someone had to say it,' said Deano, our large, mustachioed Protection Command Officer. We'd all been probationers together and had remained close for a time, but the group had fragmented over the last couple of years, Deano and Patchy having kids, and me changing my career trajectory.

It was the first time any of them had been to the flat. They looked about themselves curiously, maybe wondering if it had been such a clever idea to bring a dog for me to share in the cramped living space.

I sat back and listened to their arguments about the latest cop shows, ripping them apart and guessing at resolutions. And there was a lot of arguing about the rules of poker. We took turns screwing up the deals, betting out of turn, and showing our cards out of turn. At one point, I beat Patchy's full house with four sevens, but it took a while to work out who'd won.

'That's surprising,' Bill said. 'A full house seems like such a better hand.'

Kim had her phone in her hand, checking the rankings. 'Four of a kind wins.'

'Yeah?' Patchy asked. 'According to what website?'

'Do you want me to check a different website?' Kim asked.

'How about a different checker?'

'You don't trust me?'

'Not when it comes to you and Mike.'

Patchy tended to get belligerent after a few drinks. I always found it fascinating to see, a complete personality transplant. I was happy to leave it alone, but Kim snapped, 'What's that supposed to mean?'

The mood of the evening could have changed, but Rellers deftly swooped in. 'Well, you *did* get him a dog,' she said, nudging Kim in the ribs and Patchy out of the conversation.

'The dog is from all of us,' Kim said. 'Because we're all such considerate friends.'

'So I've got you all to blame?' I asked.

The dancing dog had tired himself out and was now in his bed staring into space.

'Now, that's zen,' Deano said. 'That dog could teach you a lot.' We'd both folded our hands. He took the opportunity to show me what a kibble hunt was. 'It's character building for pets if you throw their dried food around so they have to hunt for it. If you make it too easy, he'll go all flat and lifeless.'

'Is that what your wife says?' It slipped out. Deano looked up at me. Patchy slapped the table, laughing. I shrugged. 'Someone had to say it.'

The dog would snooze in his bed, then awake and remember he was with company and have a dance. He seemed comforted that we were there but didn't want to come too near any of us. He'd approach you, taking a closer sniff, but if you put out your hand to him, he'd dance away. It was understandable he'd want to keep his distance from people.

DESPITE MY FOUR-OF-A-KIND WIN, I went out of the game

shortly thereafter, before anyone else. I stood up to stretch my legs. Kim joked, 'Off to bed then?'

'Would you mind?' I asked. 'You guys feel free to hang around and gamble all night. In my house.'

'Second time you said *house*,' Deano said. 'Not really a house, is it?'

That set Patchy off into peals of laughter. That caused the dog to stir and dance his merry dance. The gang cheered for the dancing dog, which egged him on.

Bill was up, pointing his camera at the thing, unsuccessfully trying to take a photo. 'He's too fast and dark. He's just a black blur, *black as night on a moonless night*.'

'I approve of the *Twin Peaks* reference,' I said.

'You *have* to keep him,' Deano said. 'Look at that face. When the first dog walked up to the first man beside a campfire, offering companionship in exchange for food, I bet he had a mug like that.'

'If you're so enamoured…' I began.

'Already have one, and two kids,' he interrupted. 'But if you need a sitter from time to time, drop him round.'

I sighed and got everyone a fresh round of drinks, and sat at the table while the others played.

'Getting anywhere finding out who tried to fry our pup's previous owner?' Bill asked.

I filled them in on how far I'd got, minus the personal melodrama.

'Do you think Derek O'Mara started the fire?' Deano asked. 'Revenge for Catherine's suicide?'

'Sounds like he hates Neddy enough,' Kim said.

'From what I hear about him,' Rellers said, 'it seems to be the way he takes care of his problems.'

'I don't know if it is,' I said.

That caused every face at the table to look up at me.

'I mean, I spoke to him,' I said. 'Age seems to have mellowed him.'

'You *spoke* to Derek O'Mara?' Kim asked.

I shrugged and nodded. 'He's pretty relaxed,' I said, trying to defuse her alarm.

'Must have been one hell of a chat you had together,' she said.

'Maybe someone's trying to get to Derek,' Rellers said, moving the conversation along. I was grateful for that. 'Threatening him by having a go at his family, unknowing that he hates his son's guts.'

'Or trying to get to Donsaw,' Kim said. '*He's* the one with the true blood connection, and he's the one who wants it looked into, even if Neddy doesn't.'

'Just get them all in a room with us standing guard, ready to make the arrest when you pluck out the culprit,' Bill said. 'You go through the case, drop a few truth nuggets and wait for someone's story to fall apart.'

'I will fulfil my dream of doing that one day,' I said. 'I don't think this is the case though.'

Rellers eventually won everyone's chips. 'I win the pot, but Mike gets a dog,' she said. 'Who's the real winner?'

'It's a tricky question,' I said. 'You get hard cash and I get a life-changing responsibility.'

I was dead tired at this point and didn't have the fight in me to reject the dog. Maybe that had been their plan all along. But it was going to be more effort to keep a dog than to summon a little fight and insist Kim or one of the gang take the dog with them. I braced myself. 'So let's be serious. You can't leave him here.'

'That's between you and Kim,' Bill said.

'Way to pass on the buck,' Rellers said.

'No, he's right,' Kim said. 'Leave him to me.' She'd made

her way over to the sofa and was sitting in a very relaxed position while everyone else was putting on coats and heading to the door.

I said some goodbyes at the door, careful not to let the dog escape. The commotion had him dancing.

They left. I looked at Kim. She was smiling strangely. By strange, I mean her expression had a seductive, affectionate quality. In all the years I'd known her, she'd never given me a look like that. It was killer.

'What?' I said.

She got up and slowly walked towards me. She stood before me, still with that smile. She held my chin. 'I like the five o'clock shadow look.'

'Thanks,' I mumbled.

And she kissed me. It was quick, soft and utterly sweet. 'He's going to need a walk before you go to bed,' she said.

12

Still with that strange, killer smile, Kim picked up her coat and let herself out before I could think of a response.

Listening to her footsteps on the stairs, I entertained many schoolboy emotions before the dog distracted me. After enjoying all that company, he was still, looking at me with that long, sad face, his ears and tail drooping low. I reached out to him but he backed away. I played a little kibble hunt, which got his tail wagging again, and I lured him in to attach the lead to his collar. I took him for a quick walk up and down the road, and had to clean up his business — so much fun.

Back home, I made a home for him in the office, ruffled his fur, said goodnight to him and left a low light on. I played another kibble hunt to occupy him while I did my evening admin, brushing my teeth, dressing down to my boxers and pulling out the bed.

I lay back in the dark. My lips felt different now that Kim had pressed hers against them. I listened to the scuff of Cooper's paws on the floor as he walked around the flat in the darkness. Yes, I'd decided to name him after Agent Cooper in my half-consciousness, in honour of Bill's *Twin Peaks* quote — *black as night on a moonless night*. Although, it wasn't quite true of him. He had a tuft of white on his chest that looked like a rather dapper necktie. Maybe something in his handsome face and dark hair reminded me of Kyle MacLachlan.

I listened to the scuffing of paws as he restlessly paced around until he or I fell asleep.

He awoke with the dawn, paws up on my bed and nuzzling my face. I reached out to pat him, but he was off, a shoe in his mouth, dancing around. Do you even pat a dog, or do you pet a dog? It was interesting that he never barked. Maybe he'd had it beaten out of him.

I grabbed some clothes from a drawer and had to dress standing on the bed. He was prone to take any item off the floor that would fit in his mouth to dance around with.

It was 5am, early for me, and my head was pounding, a condition that would have been avoided with an extra couple of hours sleep. But I had a potentially new lifestyle on the horizon here and there wasn't much I could think to do to avoid it. It was what it was. I'd knocked on Neddy's door, saw what he was doing to this little fur ball, told Kim, and now I had a dog.

I picked up his lead. He came to attention. He seemed pretty relaxed about his sudden uprooting and new situation. Did he differentiate me from Neddy?

We walked a few minutes to the entrance of Highgate Woods. It never occurred to me how close I was to such a treasure of nature. Surrounded by woodland, it was hard to believe you were in London. Lots of dog walkers were around, their dogs off their leads. Cooper was straining at his lead and I was worried about strangling him, but I couldn't risk losing him on day one.

I didn't know what to do about him. I felt shy about calling Kim after that surprise kiss she'd had in store for me, and that had me in check mate. I was taking him for a second walk, and I seemed able to clear up his business, and he seemed okay in the flat.

The way I saw it, my life could have ended two nights ago. I had little right to be here. Then fate had immediately given unto me a dog to look after. I didn't feel like I had a right to argue. I couldn't say I wasn't in a position to look after a dog, that I wasn't a dog person. I wasn't anyone. I was a clean slate. Any other day in my life — hard as it would have been — I'd have denied Kim and rejected Cooper. I think.

The dappled sunlight decorated the ground before us. Fresh morning air in my lungs, and lack of a hangover, I felt strangely recovered from my actions in Soho.

I got to thinking about the case, was grateful there was more to it than there originally seemed, something to sink my teeth into. It was hard not to believe Derek. He didn't seem like he was trying to hide anything. Our interaction had been nothing if not authentic.

I needed to talk to my employer again.

I got home, waited until an appropriate hour, and started trying Donsaw's number. I repeatedly got an automated message — not a dissimilar experience to trying to contact Neddy. I gave up, sprinkled some kibble around to distract Cooper and went to see him in person.

I closed the door behind me and heard Cooper's whine — he'd realised I'd left him behind. Goodness, I couldn't do with that heartache every time I left the house.

I could have walked in the pleasant weather, but I

thought I'd make the time away from Coops as short as possible. I drove Merkel the few minutes to Donsaw's residence.

Fitzroy park was a quiet, private road, like a countryside village with humongous houses, all of which would have views of the Heath and everything beyond. Donsaw's house was a sprawling, Mock-Tudor affair, A-frame roofs jutting out of each other at different levels like an intricate gingerbread house.

It was set back behind a garden and a tall, spiky grill gate. The unwelcoming fence and a 'beware of the dog' sign were incongruous with the natural beauty of the surrounding area.

I pressed the buzzer at the gate entrance. No answer.

Don't ask me why. A feeling, or maybe I had no where else to go. I stubbornly kept pressing the buzzer.

No answer, not even the bark of a dog. I had more luck simply trying the gate. It wasn't locked. I was taking quite a gamble on my instinct there was no dog.

I walked along a would-be elegant gravel path and would have felt like I was taking a turn in a Jane Austen novel. But the garden was neglected and overgrown.

The front door was ajar. I nudged it open and entered.

Spacious and elegant, the kind of house where Poirot might summon all the residents into a room and pluck out a murderer. But it seemed deserted. Throughout the hall were piles of newspapers that hadn't been thrown out. And if Poirot ever entered, the smell of mould and damp, and even urine, would have made him turn on his heel and declare that whatever murderous business was happening, it was no business of his.

'Mr Donsaw?' I called, my voice echoing against the wood-panelled walls lined with portraits of recent ancestors with muted expressions looking out from their canvases.

There was a door to my right. I left it alone for now and followed the hall in front of me. I peeked into a room to my left, so large it looked empty, though it contained a leather sofa and chairs, with a built-in library of dusty books.

I bypassed a staircase. An open doorway wound around to a room that would have been behind the first closed door I'd left alone. This was a more comfortably sized room. It could have been a cosy dining room if there had been a table, a reading room if there had been any books, a living room if there was any semblance of life. The room contained four cracked but comfortable-looking leather armchairs. It also contained a mini bar and drinks cabinet, comprising a lot of empty bottles, though there were plenty with drink still in them, all expensive labels. I suppose that made it the drinking room.

I'd made myself take in all these details before making myself look at the figure sitting in one of the chairs. It was Edward Donsaw. He wasn't moving, and he didn't look or smell too well.

He was wearing the same style of clothes he'd worn in my office — light coloured, smart-casual, but now they were worn and shapeless.

I was sure he was dead.

He had a two-day beard growing on his regal face. His eyes were bloodshot and staring dead ahead. But then they flickered over to where I was standing. The shock of it shot a bolt of pain through my back.

I took a deep breath of relief despite the sour aroma emanating from the undead man, which I now recognised as the sourness of a drinker.

My new instinct — after the initial instinct of thinking

this was a dead body — was distaste, but I could hardly judge, the car wreck of a life I'd been living the last couple of days. It was as if what I saw around me was a Dorian Gray-like reflection of my soul. The sight and smell made me want to take immediate control of my life, or at least do a spring clean.

I saw myself in him, this situation, this squalor, except that my entire flat would have easily fit into any one of these rooms. This could be how I'd end up if I let myself drink more regularly, or if I didn't just end it. I wondered if it really had been a lucky break that Ricky hadn't been a professional.

I could see a bottle of half-empty Glen Drumnadrochit sitting at a reachable distance on his left-hand side and a half-full tumbler in his hand. There was no recognition in his face, but he spat the words, 'Where have you *been*?'

'Mr Donsaw,' I said. 'Are you okay?' It was a stupid question. He didn't reply. I went on, 'I tried to contact you by phone, then I thought I'd just come round. Your door was open and I came in to see if everything was alright.'

'Did you bring a bottle?' It was a crazy, hoarse voice, nothing like the velvety, upper-class tones he used in my office.

'A bottle? Mr Donsaw, I'm Michael Seferis.'

'I don't care who you are!' he shouted, which was surprising.

'Okay,' I said in a soothing tone. 'Mr Donsaw, is there anyone else here with you?'

'What's it to you?'

'Is there someone who looks after you?'

'Look after me? Who here is going to look after me? I'm surrounded by imbeciles! I sent you out to get a bottle and you can't even get that right.'

I could see he had enough whisky to keep him in a haze for the rest of the day, but the fact he was demanding a drink he already had seemed the least of our problems. The most pressing issue was that he'd seemed to have lost his mind.

'I think you've got me mixed up with someone else, Mr Donsaw. Has someone gone to the shops for you?' I looked around. If he had someone taking care of that much, why didn't they clean the place?

'Oh yes,' he said without inflection. 'I got you mixed up with the maid.'

A maid? Was he crazy *and* screwing with me?

'Mr Donsaw, I'm Mike Seferis. You hired me to look into the fire at Neddy's house.'

'Neddy! He's a good boy. Better than the layabouts I have with me here.'

A reference to the sons Kim had told me about. Or the maid?

'Right, Neddy,' I said. 'He's in trouble. You asked me to help him.'

He gazed at me vacantly. An optimistic man would take it as an invitation to continue.

I continued, 'I was told you're more than just a friend of the family. I was told you're his blood-grandfather.'

He was whipped into a rage. 'My own flesh and blood!' he shouted, emphasising each word.

He stared his rage into me and, my god, I saw Neddy in there, the angry, ugly, squashed features. 'Why don't you leave the boy alone?' he shouted. 'Haven't you done enough damage!'

'Hey!' I shouted back, hoping to shock him into some form of sanity. It got his attention at least. 'I'm Mike Seferis. You think Neddy's in trouble because there was a fire. You came to see me in my office and you paid me a cheque. Do you remember that? It's my job to find out what happened.'

'Sounds like a shit job,' he said, calm again. Despite everything, he still managed to take me by surprise; he was starting to make sense.

'It's better not to know things,' he said. 'It's better to know nothing.'

I sighed. 'You might be right.' I bent close towards him to give it one more try. 'But I'm a detective, and you came to me for help.'

It hit home. I saw the light of recognition make his eyes widen and his mouth gape. I saw Neddy again. It unsettled me. What a pair these two made.

He looked around himself, disorientated, but a hell of a lot more orientated than he had been a few seconds ago.

'My own flesh and blood,' he said again, not shouting this time but, again, emphasising each word. He went on to say, 'Everyone wants the past to stay buried.'

'Who are you and what are you doing here?' The voice was accusatory. I turned around. A corpulent, sweaty man in a worn suit stood in a power stance. He had a strange haircut, a full head of hair slimed flat across his head so it looked like a bad comb-over.

I'd seen an online image of one of Donsaw's sons. It wasn't the man in front of me, which likely meant this was Robert Donsaw. He looked ready to charge.

I showed my palms. Then I slowly pulled out my ID. 'I'm Mike Seferis, a private detective in the employment of this man. I've not been able to get through to the phone number he gave me, so I came to see him and found him here in this state.'

'A detective? Investigating what?'

'Well, that's between me and Mr Donsaw.' I looked at

Donsaw. He stared straight ahead at nothing. 'Though I don't know if it's even that.'

'How did you get in here?'

'The door was open.'

'And the gate?'

'Unlocked.'

A smug expression of victory flashed across the man's face. 'I'm ex-police,' I said. 'It's in my nature to check inside a house with an open door, especially if I'm working for the occupant.' It was weak, but it wiped the expression off his face.

'You look like a hustler to me.'

'He came to *my* office. He asked me to look into a sensitive matter. When he didn't answer his phone, I got worried,' I lied. 'I was even more worried when the door was open. Seeing the state he's in, I don't think my worry was unwarranted.'

'What is this sensitive matter?'

'I'm not at liberty to say.'

'I'm his son, and this is my house, and his business is my business.'

'Whose business is it to get this place cleaned and some care for this man?'

'That's a wonder why you don't mind your own business.'

He had a point. Last time I made a comment like that I ended up adopting a dog. I didn't want Edward Donsaw moving in with me as well. 'Take it easy,' I said. 'I met Mr Donsaw on Friday. He was charming and coherent. It's a shock to see him in this state. You're Robert Donsaw?'

After a hesitant pause, he defiantly answered, 'I am.'

I gestured at Donsaw senior. 'How can this be the same man I spoke to before? Is it drink or something else?'

Robert stared at me. It wasn't the friendliest of expressions. I didn't think I was going to get an answer, and anyway, Edward Donsaw himself finally piped up, explosively. 'Don't talk about me like I'm not here! *This* is me. I'm not one of those sham paintings on the wall.'

The outburst was piercing. I rode the urge to massage my ears.

'Look! You've put him in a state,' Robert said.

'He was like that when I got here.'

'Where have you *been*?' Donsaw shouted, as if he'd regressed back to the moment I'd first entered.

'Out,' Robert said tiresomely.

'There's nothing out there!'

'There's a hell of a lot more out there than in here!' Robert shouted back. 'Did you employ this man to dig up our past?'

'Ha! Nice choice of words!'

For the first time since our introduction, Robert's manner lost all its hostility. He was speechless, like he'd just taken a surprise slap in the face.

I gave him a moment to recover. When he didn't, I spoke. 'Look, I didn't realise what a sick man he was. He was coherent. He wrote me a normal cheque, and I started working a very normal case. Now I feel like I was wrong to take his money.'

Robert Donsaw looked at me, timidly, like a child who'd been told off by a parent. 'Don't worry about that.'

'Don't worry about ten thousand pounds?'

Robert Donsaw scoffed. I'd managed to give him his essence back. 'For your troubles. But, please, it ends here.'

'You have a brother, William.'

'I don't want you bothering him! You just said you felt

guilty about taking my father's money and I asked you to stop pestering my family.'

'Under the circumstances, I think I'd better tell you everything.' I paused. This was Donsaw senior's opportunity to protest and give away any lucidity he might have. No words were spoken. I continued. 'There's a young man named Neddy Mara in trouble with the law. Your father wanted to help him, said he was a friend of the family, and hired me. Do you know him?'

Robert Donsaw's expression was blank, too blank. 'I don't.'

I looked at Donsaw senior one last time. He, too, gave nothing away, looking off into the distance.

'Mr Donsaw,' I said to the son. 'I apologise for the intrusion. I'll let myself out.' And I did. Robert Donsaw didn't see me to the door. Neither did his father for that matter.

13

The sunlight hurt my eyes after the darkness of the Sam Shepherd play I'd just taken part in. I wanted to get into the safe, sane bubble of my car before thinking everything over. When I got into the Mini, however, the reason I'd driven instead of walked occurred to me. I'd left a crying puppy at home.

I drove home mostly with thoughts of the dog in my mind, though still with the smell of rancid cheese in my nostrils from the mansion on Hampstead Heath. I could hear Cooper whining as I came into the building and I jogged up the stairs to open my door. The whining stopped and the silent wiggling dance commenced.

I had a lot of love for this little mutt right now. After seeing the madness and dramas that humans created, this guy was a pure soul. And it had been a human who'd mistreated him, an unofficial member of the Donsaw family no less.

I decided I didn't want to leave him alone again, but I wasn't sure how I was going to swing that. Could I afford to pay a dog sitter while I was out and about, one of those people I saw walking around the neighbourhood with a gang of dogs all tied to a lead? Would I trust anyone else to look after him? 'I didn't ask for this,' I said aloud, in a friendly tone Cooper could enjoy.

I took a seat, watched the dog wriggle around, and mulled over the Donsaws. What was the difference between Donsaw and me? Maybe not such a leap. If I didn't change my ways, my lifestyle, my opinion about people, if I let misery and hatred fill me, I could be a babbling madman screaming for drink, unable to see I had a bottle an arm's length away.

'I bet this never happened to Kinsey Millhone,' I said to Cooper. 'There were plenty of people who wanted her off a case, but I can't think of any who'd forgotten they'd put her on one in the first place. You should have seen him. He was bonkers. Can mere alcoholism do that to a man?'

Cooper didn't answer, but he seemed to enjoy the repartee.

'Anyway,' I said. 'Looks like I'm off the case.' But I wondered. Which one of Donsaw's sons was Neddy's real father? Did Neddy know? Robert was adamant I not talk to William. Was he protecting him? Would I ever hear from Donsaw senior again?

That moment with Ricky and the gun wasn't far from my mind. I'd been determined to charge into the abyss, put an end to everything during a cold, grey summer in the middle of a case I hadn't solved. I held the thought at arm's length and focused on the case. I looked online and reminded myself that William Donsaw was credited with being the founder of the London Classical Piano Festival. On the 'About' page, there was an alumni list. By each name were one or more job descriptions and other achievements they'd made. William was at the bottom, his only credit 'Co-founder'. It was as if he was the only one not showing off, or he was only reluctantly being mentioned on the alumni list.

I CALLED the number on the website. A female voice answered. 'This is going back a few years,' I said. 'I'm writing a book about William Donsaw. He's on your website as one of your founders. Has anyone been there for that amount of time I could talk to?'

She ummed and ahhed. 'You could try contacting George Rawson-Hill, one of our patrons. He's not hands-on with the festival anymore, but I think he's been around since the beginning.'

I called the number she gave me and spoke to a remote secretary, who put me through to another secretary, who put me through to the man himself. I gave him the same line about being a writer. 'Anything at all you can tell me about William Donsaw would be useful.'

'Ah yes, fine old fellow,' Rawson-Hill said. 'I used to see him at the Oriental Club. I'm out of the city and not in great health these days. I don't get there as much as I'd like to see the old chaps.'

I imagined him in dressing gown and slippers, smoking a big cigar. Rawson-Hill told a few anecdotes about the Oriental, like one about a fine old general known by all as 'the man with the scar' who'd gotten away with killing his wife.

I made affirmative sounds. It was one of my weaknesses — allowing older folk to gush on like this. Maybe it was the well-brought-up, polite kid in me. He'd lose the thread of each story and would prompt himself to start another. I let a few more minutes pass before utilising a pause and asking, 'Do you have any anecdotes about William and his family?'

'William?'

'William Donsaw.'

There was an uncertain pause. Now I imagined him with a crystal cut glass of Scotch in his hand instead of the cigar, and not his first of the day.

'You said he was one of the fellows you knew at the Oriental.'

'I did?'

'He co-founded the London Classical Piano Festival.'

'He did?'

'Were you involved in the London Classical Piano Festival?'

'Yes! I founded it! Me and one of the chaps at the club, had a passion for Elgar.'

'You and William Donsaw?'

'Perhaps. Quiet boy, kept to himself.'

'Sure. Anything else you can tell me about him?'

'Let's see. Oh yes. He was seeing that Amaryllis girl for a while.'

'Amaryllis?'

'Such a sweetheart. I knew her mother, Rose. Wonderful woman. We had such times. She was such fun. I was very hopeful for them, but it didn't work out in the end.'

'Really? I'd love to speak to Amaryllis.'

'Ah, well, it's rather tragic I'm afraid.'

'Oh?'

'Yes, she was in an accident.'

'Oh dear. I'm sorry to hear that.'

'What's that now?'

'I'm sorry to hear Amaryllis was in an accident.'

'Was she? No, I'm thinking of the Balvenie girl. Tragic thing, crashed her car, she went through the windshield.'

'It's tragic. But what about Amaryllis?'

'Amaryllis, I believe she's at Classical Radio.'

He went on, and I let him, too polite and unable to catch a pause to cut him off. I learned about *his* love of Elgar and more.

When I finally let George Rawson-Hill go, we'd been on the phone for an hour. After a deep breath and a cup of tea, I endeavoured to find out if Amaryllis was a lead, or even real.

A LITTLE ONLINE searching and I came across one Amaryllis Jones. She was no longer with Classical Radio, but they'd kept her information on their website, along with her job descriptions over the years. She'd done everything from reviewing to cataloguing to digital tasks.

A little more online searching and I had her phone number. The line was busy first time round, but second time, a genteel voice answered.

'Amaryllis?'

'Yes.'

'I'm Mike Seferis, a private investigator. I'm looking to gather information on the Donsaw family.'

'The Donsaw family?' she repeated slowly. 'Goodness, whatever for?'

'Someone started a fire and their names have come up during an investigation.'

'Was anyone hurt?'

'Fortunately not. Just property damage.'

'What a curious situation. I don't see how I can help. It's been such a long time since I've been in contact with that family, decades.'

'I'm happy to come and see you, if you could spare the time.'

'Come to my home?'

'Unless you'd like to meet somewhere, but I assume your home would be the least inconvenient thing for you.'

A face-to-face wasn't going to get me any further on the case, and driving to Harrow was going to be a pain in the arse, but after my surreal glimpse into the Donsaws' lives, and even my comical talk with Rawson-Hill, I wanted to see in person someone who came into contact with this strange class of people and their environment.

But it was rich for me to be calling *them* strange, because then I asked, 'Are you averse to cocker spaniels?'

'Excuse me?'

'I've recently acquired a dog and I don't like to leave him alone. I was thinking of bringing him with me.'

'Is he house-trained?'

I hesitated. 'I don't know. Sorry, it was a stupid question.'

'Bless you,' she said, like I was a boy scout selling biscuits at her door. Badly. 'Of course you can bring your cocker spaniel, though I live in Harrow,' like that was going to be a deterrent, which it was to an extent.

I sighed. My professionalism was going out the window. 'I can be there in an hour.'

'Gosh, well, it's your hour,' she said.

I agreed it was and asked for her address.

HARROW IS NORTH-WEST OF LONDON. I think of it as a commuter suburb. Maybe residents would disagree. Its claim to fame is that, up on the hill — Harrow-on-the-Hill as it were — was Harrow School, one of the country's big, posh private schools, where future politicians, amongst other things, were bred.

The school owns a lot of the on-the-Hill area, protecting

it from modernisation. It was quaint, with Georgian architecture, not unlike Highgate village. In fact, the slope of the small neighbourhood streets was even steeper.

Amaryllis's address was on-the-Hill. I parked in a space a couple of blocks from her place, fearing my hand-brake wouldn't be enough to keep Merkel from rolling down the hill.

I left Cooper in the car. He watched me with his sad eyes from the window.

I found the house, rang the bell and a woman, with hard features and a stern expression that reminded me of an old headmistress I'd had, opened the door.

She tilted her head in playful disappointment, the headmistress in her melting away when she smiled. 'You left the cocker spaniel at home?'

'I left him in the car. I didn't think it was appropriate. It's just that... it's day one of being a dog owner. He's been locked in a small flat on his own all day.'

'And you left him in the car?'

'... Yes.'

'Why don't you get him? Dogs feel very vulnerable when they're locked in cars.'

I tried to think of an objection, then I said, 'Okay,' and went to get Cooper.

I returned with the dog. 'He's darling,' Amaryllis said. She tried to pet him, or pat him, and he wriggled away.

She bade me enter. Through a hallway, I could see a conservatory and sizable garden. Cooper was straining at his lead. 'You should let him go,' she said.

'Are you sure?'

'He just wants to investigate this strange new world, then he'll settle down.'

I unleashed him and he shot off like a rocket, just like he

had at my place, to sniff every nook and cranny.

We entered a living room containing a couple of wooden chairs, a worn rug under our feet, and a sofa against the wall that looked like a wet towel thrown in a heap on the floor. Built-in bookcases covered almost every part of the far wall, the books faded and tattered.

An upright piano stood against another wall. A cello rested beside it.

Amaryllis sat in the wooden chair; I made myself as comfortable as I could on the sofa. Cooper joined us, laying his nose on his front paws, looking away from us.

'You play the cello?' I asked.

'You sound surprised.'

'It's just that, your name...'

She smiled. 'I was named after Amaryllis Fleming. Do you follow music?'

'Not really,' I said. She waited for an explanation, so I went on. '*The Living Daylights.*'

'Excuse me? The James Bond film?'

'Yes, well, it's a short story. The author, Ian Fleming, his mother, Eve, had an affair with Augustus John, the painter. They had a daughter together, Amaryllis, out of wedlock, which was tricky in those days. So, she was told she was a foster daughter until she became an adult.'

'I didn't know that,' Amaryllis said.

I regretted starting the anecdote, but I had to see it through now. 'Her brother — half-brother — paid tribute to her in *The Living Daylights*. While being a sniper, Bond sees a cellist in another window and says something like: *There's something indecent about a bulbous ungainly instrument between splayed thighs. That girl Amaryllis managed to look elegant.*'

Amaryllis laughed. 'That's a bizarre line.'

'Uh huh.'

'And a bizarre piece of knowledge to have off the top of your head.'

'I know a lot of useless things,' I said.

'Well, my parents were fans of Amaryllis Fleming, and perhaps they just liked the name, but they encouraged me to pursue music.'

She was so warm, I had to hold back the urge to mention Alison, that she played so beautifully, yet I never knew *what* she was playing. Now she was gone, I'd been left with no knowledge of the music I'd come to love.

She made me a very milky tea. I thought of apologising and saying I actually took it black to receive something more drinkable, but I soldiered through.

'So, you're interested in the Donsaw family?' she asked.

'Just looking to find out anything I can.'

'Because there's been a fire?'

I can't say what it was, but I trusted her. I was asking a lot of her and was prepared for full disclosure on my own part. I started at the beginning, when a dapper Edward Donsaw came to me and over paid me to look into a scrape a 'friend of the family' had got themselves into.

I got as far as telling her, 'The facts weren't adding up, so I tried to call Donsaw to ask him what I was supposed to make of all this. When I couldn't get hold of him, I went to his home. He was an incoherent, raving drunk. His son, Robert, appeared and told me to mind my own business and, oh yes, keep the money I'd received.'

'But you decided against minding your own business,' Amaryllis said playfully.

'I don't have much else on.'

'Except this little fellow,' Amaryllis said, again with her sweet smile. Cooper caught on he was being talked about and did his wriggle around the room routine, coming close to us, then wriggling away again.

'I guess I need to work on my priorities,' I said. 'I'm just not the kind of person to take a pay off without at least knowing more of the story.'

'I can appreciate that, but I've had nothing to do with them in... goodness, something like thirty years.'

'But you have had something to do with them at least. I need something to go on, some clue about their dynamic, what they were like, even thirty years ago.'

I told her how her name came up, after speaking to a rather rambling and disorientated Rawson-Hill. 'He said, William had been seeing Amaryllis.'

'Yes, William and I were an item. We met at a performance of Beethoven's piano concertos at Wigmore Hall. I was there with a girlfriend. William had pulled Robert along. Robert started talking to us at the interval, and I was drawn to William, the quiet one with a passion for the music.

'We went to performances together. I encouraged him to follow his passion and he founded the London Classical Piano Festival. A lot of it was done without the signing of papers, so, after a couple of years, a few of the people he'd reeled in for help wrestled ownership of the festival from him.'

'George Rawson-Hill?' I asked. It didn't concern me, but I knew it somehow and wanted to confirm it.

Amaryllis nodded. 'A simple power struggle, and William wasn't interested in power, he was too rich. He loved the music, and the situation depressed him. Maybe he could have done something legally, but he didn't want to. He wasn't a businessman.'

'What did he do after that?'

'Nothing. He withdrew and, like his brother, spent most of his time eating and drinking at his club. Then he withdrew from me. After a significant period together, he said we shouldn't see each other anymore. I don't even remember the conversation we had now. Maybe it was my ego, but I was sure his father had had a word with him. I think I confronted him and asked him outright if that's what happened, and he didn't deny it. Something like that. I remember thinking, all that money, all that privilege, yet... what a poisonous place to come from. I was earning enough to take care of both of us and, without the comforts of his lifestyle, perhaps he could have done something extraordinary.' She sighed. 'Well, it's ancient history now.'

'You never met the great Donsaw senior in person?'

'I never had the honour.'

'Did you cross paths with other friends or family?'

'Friends... no. There were his *good old fellows* at his club, but, being a woman, I wasn't allowed in there. We'd sometimes spend time with Robert and whoever was on his arm.'

'Was there a woman called Catherine Moore?'

Amaryllis lit up. 'Goodness, yes. The burlesque performer! She had a wonderful, fifties-chic look, her dark hair always impeccably styled.' Her amusement faded. 'She was seeing Robert. She didn't stand a chance. I thought, if a middle-class girl like myself isn't good enough for the Donsaw family, how's *this* going to play out? She was fun, a real bohemian. She was with the more outgoing brother. Robert saw her perform somewhere, and she and him became an item. Then she was in a low-budget play that was successful, so she became a serious actress and did a lot of TV work.'

'What happened with her and Robert?'

'She disappeared from the crowd, quite abruptly. I

suspect the same happened as with me and William, the elder Donsaw sticking his oar in and threatening disinheritance. It's funny. On paper, they didn't seem like a very serious couple, her colourful past and his stifling background, the fact their relationship seemed to centre around drinks and parties. She seemed like the latest evidence of Robert's playboy lifestyle. But after she left the picture, he changed. He was more serious, depressed really. The womanising ended. Yes,' she said vacantly, as if these thoughts were coming to her for the first time. 'He was never quite the same after Catherine. I sometimes wonder what became of her.'

I felt reluctant to lay the sad story on this amiable lady, but I did. 'Catherine married Derek O'Mara, a player in the Soho underworld who had a soft spot for her. So he tells me, she was with child. It was Robert's. Derek had a soft spot for Catherine and he brought Neddy up as his own. The patriarch, Edward, knew about the child. Perhaps someone was paid off. Perhaps he threatened to disinherit Robert, or perhaps Catherine was even scared of something.'

'Scared?' Amarylis asked.

'Yes. Derek said she went to him because she knew he would keep her safe. From what? I don't know. Can you think of any reason Edward Donsaw should be feared?'

'Goodness, no. The only power he wielded was his chequebook.'

'It's funny you'd say that,' I said. 'Edward let over a decade pass, then he came back into Neddy's life. I don't know what he said to the teenager, but he started bankrolling him. This action sent an already rebellious youth off the rails. He was suddenly independently wealthy and he treated his parents with disdain.

'I don't know if his behaviour is solely to blame, but he was troubled, and a burden. A year or so ago, Catherine took her own life.'

'Oh my god.' Amaryllis hands covered her mouth.

'I'm sorry to have to tell you,' I said.

'How can that be? She was so... alive.'

I nodded and let the silence stretch.

'What was Robert like?' Amaryllis finally asked. Almost wistful.

'We didn't meet under the most pleasant circumstances. He caught me digging into his family's history and he was angry. Physically, he was overweight, a drinker's face.'

Amaryllis looked surprised. 'No evidence of a handsome young playboy?'

'Not that I could see.'

She snorted. 'No one was good enough for Edward Donsaw's boys, so he drove every woman away. Now they're the three musketeers growing old together.'

'Maybe that's what he wanted,' I said.

'Except that I imagine it's all a bit more *What Ever Happened to Baby Jane?* than *Frasier*.'

'It *did* feel like a horror film,' I said. 'He seems to have lost his mind to the bottle.'

'Very sad.'

'Did William ever mention his mother?'

'The mother,' Amaryllis said. 'There was mention of a mother. She left William's father and attached herself to a younger man. I recall something like, this other man had no *standing* or wealth of his own, and that *really* got to Edward. Imagine being left for a man with no *standing*.'

'Unthinkable,' I said.

Amaryllis searched her mind for more details. 'She was more interested in society and her young man than her sons, and they never had much contact with her. They were still in short trousers when she left. She wanted a divorce, but I don't think Edward wanted the scandal. He financed her and her lover's lavish lifestyle, and, for her part, few people knew about the arrangement. Explains a lot, don't you think?'

'That big house of theirs doesn't seem to have had a woman's touch in years,' I said.

Amaryllis raised her eyebrows. 'Are you saying it wasn't clean? Ergo, a cleaner or maid hasn't done their duty, which is where a woman should come into the equation?'

'Um, what about you, Amaryllis? This has nothing to do with the case, but how did you come to work for Classical Radio and end up living in this nice house in Harrow?'

'I don't usually expound about my life, Michael, but bringing little Cooper with you is a very disarming tactic. I went to school with a music scholarship. I moved here because I was teaching music at Harrow. I made connections through William's project and that's how I got involved with Classical Radio. I did that for a while. Now I teach privately and work with choirs and things like that. I never married. William was the time I felt most connected and you know that story.'

I liked Amaryllis's warmth and openness, but I didn't know if it was worth the drive. The visit hadn't taken care of the curiosity I'd had, because she was an ordinary woman who hadn't been allowed into that crazy world I was trying to understand.

I made a little small talk, thanked her for her time and she saw me to the door. 'I hope it was helpful,' she said. 'Thinking about the past like that wasn't much fun, but Cooper made it worthwhile.'

Maybe he *was* the dynamic partner I needed.

14

I hit rush hour and was in for a long drive home. Cooper sat next to me, perfectly zen, staring out the window. I ruffled his ears.

'I can imagine Edward Donsaw telling William that Amaryllis was below him and he shouldn't see her anymore, despite her awesome name. It can't have been as easy with Robert. Maybe a substantial pay off would have been made for that to happen.'

Cooper said nothing.

But for Catherine to see Edward as a dangerous, sinister presence? I still couldn't make any sense of that.

I said to Cooper, 'So Edward Donsaw pushed away and effectively disowned a child that was his own flesh and blood. And he shouted that at me so meaningfully when I saw him: *my own flesh and blood.* He took away Robert's opportunity for fatherhood, and it ate him up inside and ate away at the family until they became the sorry sight I saw this morning. He wanted to keep his sons close to him, but now there's no heir, perhaps he finally wants to connect with, or at least influence, his descendant. Now he sees his grandson is in trouble, he's throwing money and private detectives at the problem. It could be his way of making amends.'

Cooper still said nothing. Perhaps he was too close to the drama to make an objective observation.

Hunger got the better of me and, as I was in the area, I made a detour to Keany's for a sandwich. Maybe I could ask him if he knew anything about Poppy, that calculating ex-girlfriend who had plenty of motive to cause Neddy trouble.

I took Cooper in with me, figuring the establishment would be hip enough to allow dogs. I was glad to see there wasn't too much of a queue, just one young woman standing at the counter, facing Keany. Keany noticed me and waved a friendly hello.

The woman stood aside and looked over her shoulder. It was Jane. Her eyes widened, then narrowed. I swallowed my own surprise and gave her my best nonchalant nod.

'What are you doing here?' she hissed.

Surprisingly, Keany jumped to my defence. 'He's a customer.'

'That's right,' I said. 'And it's an emergency. I need a braised beef special.'

Cooper was straining at the lead and doing his dance. I thought — oh crap. Jane was looking down at him. 'That looks like Neddy's dog.'

I pursed my lips and crinkled my eyebrows, an attempt at confusion. 'You what?'

I could see her mind working. She realised it was too much of a stretch. 'Nothing.'

'It's alright to have him in here?' I asked Keany, who was slicing bread.

'Sure. You eating here?'

'I'll take it to go.'

'I'm going to the loo,' Jane said pointedly, keeping her mean eyes on me as she brushed past me.

I watched her disappear behind the toilet door at the far end of the cafe, and said, 'Friendly girl.'

'She warms the more you get to know her,' Keany said. 'Not much. I give her a discount. She and her friends go to the Barfly a lot, just around the corner.'

'Didn't Neddy have another girlfriend?' I asked. 'I mentioned I've been following the band for a while.'

'You'll have to narrow it down. He's had a few.'

'Was her name... Poppy?'

'Oh, Poppy, sure. That's a shit show. He's seeing her again right now. On the side. Jane doesn't know about it.'

He popped open a packet of crisps, looking up at me with a grin on his face. Then the grin, and the colour in his face, disappeared. It seemed as though he was looking through me. I turned around and Jane was standing there. She must have changed her mind about using the toilets.

My glance flitted from one to the other. Keany's mouth was open. I could see his mind working. Was there any way to discount what he'd just said?

Jane's face was twisted in anger like a Gorgon. It was hard to behold. 'That fucker,' she screamed, loud enough that my right eardrum started ringing.

She threw open the door so it crashed against the wall and stormed out. That got Cooper dancing. He loved a commotion.

'Jane!' Keany shouted. He went to run after her, then he stopped, hesitating. He was looking at the sandwich. He quickly sprinkled the crisps and added the last slice of bread. The man was an artist.

Then it was back to the situation at hand. He came from around the counter again, mumbling, 'Shit, she's heading down there.' He shouted, 'Darren!' to someone in a back room. 'I'm heading out. You're in charge.'

'What?'

'I've got to head out!'

'Where?'

'I... don't have time to explain. Just hold down the fort!'

'Alright.'

Now he was across the cafe and out of the door. I looked down at the sandwich. It looked finished. It looked good. It was unwrapped and unpaid for. Damn, I was hungry.

He came back in. 'Dammit. She's got into her car and she's heading north. She's going to Neddy's. I know it.'

'Need a ride?' I asked.

After a moment of surprise, he recovered. 'That... would be amazing.'

I grabbed the sandwich from behind the counter. 'Let's go.'

I tumbled Cooper into the back seat and we jumped into Merkel. Keany pointed to Jane's BMW sports car. She wasn't yet out of sight.

'There she is.'

'I'm on it.'

'Thanks for this.'

'No worries. You just sounded so serious. Think she can do any damage?'

'That's what worries me. She has marks she's made on herself. I don't know what she's capable of. It could be something dark.'

I awkwardly picked the sandwich off my lap and took a bite, my eyes on the road, of course. 'Sorry, I just took this. I was so hungry.'

'It's on the house, least I can do.'

Cooper was clambering to join us. 'He likes to ride up front,' I said. 'Could you take him, keep my sandwich safe?'

'Sure,' Keany said. He helped Cooper through, and he sat in his lap looking at the sandwich.

'Looks like Neddy's dog,' Keany said.

'Oh?' I said. 'Weird.'

'He even... has that little tuft of white on his chest.' He looked up at me then. I returned his gaze quickly and looked back at the road.

I thought for a moment. I had nothing. 'What can I say? He's a rescue.'

Keany nodded. 'I think I get what you're saying.'

We followed the sports car through Kentish Town.

'How does he do it?' I asked, hoping to shift Keany's attention from Cooper. 'Neddy and these women, I mean.'

Keany shrugged. 'I don't get women. Maybe they like his look.'

I thought about his comment about the marks Jane made on herself. Maybe the appeal of Neddy was a form of self-abuse. Isn't it in our nature to cause ourselves suffering? Poppy had told me about how she was willing to stick with him despite his abusiveness, for whatever that was worth.

The cars separating us from Jane had filtered away and we were only three cars behind her. 'Beep your horn,' Keany said.

I didn't see what that was supposed to achieve, but I did it. Keany wound down his window, put his head outside and called her name. Then he called a number on his phone. 'No answer. Doesn't even have a service to pick up messages, textbook Neddy.'

He called another number and explained what was happening to the person on the other end of the line. 'Yeah, meet us down there. That'd be good.' He said to me, 'Nathan lives in Archway; might be able to get there before we do. He and Jane have a connection. I think he could stop her from doing anything dumb.'

Just as well. A slow driver blocked us, we got caught at a traffic light and Jane pulled away.

WE ARRIVED at Neddy's house. His door was open. Jane must have let herself in with her key, then left it that way.

I double-parked. Keany jumped out. I held onto Cooper's collar and gave him the last of the sandwich so he didn't go after him. Crumbs of bread and beef were everywhere. I picked them off myself and put them in the passenger footwell. When Cooper started to busy himself there, I got out too.

Another car pulled into the street behind us. Nathan and Jude got out, and we all exchanged glances before hearing shouting coming from the house.

I followed the other three inside. All the lights were on. We followed a passageway through an open door to a bedroom, double the size of mine.

Neddy, Jane and Poppy were mid-confrontation. Poppy was wearing a green robe, Neddy only a pair of grey boxers. His torso was hairless and scrawny to the point of looking prepubescent. Tattoos covered the right side of his torso, his arms and neck so they were just a blur of colour. They were both dough-faced and blinking, as if they'd just awoken from a post-coital nap. Jane had been ugly-crying.

They looked up to take in the new arrivals. Poppy grinned at me like the cat with the cream. If anyone would have caught the glance, things could have got even trickier than they already were.

It flashed through my mind. She and Neddy were seeing

each other behind Jane's back. After I paid Neddy a visit, he talked the incident over with his illicit lover. 'Some PI has been hired to poke his nose into the fire incident.' She'd known who I was. Perhaps she'd been intrigued. That was why she'd invited me into her place without ceremony. Then she played her cute game, played the role of being questioned, saw a weakness and pounced. *Come over, come inside, have a drink, you poor thing...*

Neddy's expression went from caught-red-handed to rage when he saw me. 'What the fuck are you doing here?'

I didn't get a chance to answer. Keany rushed to my defence again. 'Don't start on him. He's a regular customer of mine.'

That was nice. I'd bought two sandwiches and gained Keany's loyalty. I had no idea what I would have said. I'd got involved in this group because I thought they were involved in a very professional arson job that outwitted the police. I didn't think that anymore. They were a bunch of dumb kids playing musical beds.

'Jane,' Nathan said. 'Are you alright?'

'No! I'm not fucking alright! They're fucking behind my back.' She turned back to Neddy. 'What's the fucking point? Are we married? Do you need to have affairs and fuck old women with more money? You're allowed to do what you want. You didn't need to string me along like a dumb cow.'

'Who are you calling old?' Poppy said. 'I'm twenty-eight.'

'Yeah,' Jane said. 'I know all about you, the snorty bitch who thinks she's an artist. You two make a great pair, screwing each other and screwing over everyone around you because you've got nothing better to do!'

Poppy looked wounded, which I found just a little bit satisfying.

'Look,' Jude said. 'I didn't feel like this was my business, but this is all such bullshit. Jane, I've seen you and Nathan together. I've seen your texts to him. You're acting all angry, but it's just... a fucking act.'

That caused a pause.

'Yeah.' Jane attempted recovery. 'But... I haven't *done* anything with him.'

She said it to Jude, but he was expressionless. He'd dropped his grenade and he was done.

It was time for the wrath of Neddy. 'WHAT? What the hell is that supposed to mean? What *have* you done?'

'Nothing,' Nathan said. 'But I love her. We were going to tell you before we let anything happen.'

'Shut up, Nathan,' Jane said.

'What?' Nathan was dumbfounded.

'Don't tell me what I want.'

Nathan had taken a hit. 'I'm... not. *You* told me you want to be with me, but you were worried about how mentally unstable Neddy is.'

'Mentally unstable?' Neddy shouted.

Poppy said to a bereft Nathan. 'She wants Neddy now she knows she can't have him. It's textbook Jane.'

'Fuck *you!*' Jane screamed, her voice warbling. 'You don't even know me.'

'What's to know? You've got the depth of salmon.'

'Jane.' Nathan hadn't given up on her.

'And you brought her here?' Jane said. 'In our bed?'

'It's not our bed,' Neddy shouted. 'I fucking bought it.'

'Oh, you *bought* it. It's all about fucking money with you. You have the money and you're the king, and we're all just players in your little circus. The bed is yours, although *I* helped bring it in here and put it together. Just so you can have a revolving door of old slags.' She got out a set of keys.

An awkward moment ensued as she extracted one. Then she threw it at Neddy.

Neddy clamped a hand on his face. 'Aw! You got me in the eye, bitch!'

'Good! Hope I blinded you.'

'You're playing around too! What's the difference between us and you?'

'He's right,' Nathan said. 'This is our chance. You felt bad about hurting him.'

'Nathan,' Jane said. 'Will you shut up?'

'Nathan.' Keany took his arm. 'Maybe we're best off out of this.'

'No!' Nathan pulled himself free. 'He fucks everything up. I've tried to be the good guy and not stir up shit, but he's screwed the girlfriend of every band member. It's his goal to screw up everything around him. He fucked Eleanor, and he fucked your ex.'

He gestured at Jude and Keany. 'What?' they shouted in unison.

'I saw it all, but I said nothing because I was in love with Jane. I wanted her to come away with me without poisoning anything. Now I don't know *what's* going on.'

'Sounds like sex addiction,' Poppy said. She nodded at Jane. 'That would explain his lack of standards.'

Jane screamed and went for her. They both crashed to the floor, along with a lamp. Neddy laughed. The rest of the band were on them, trying to pry them apart.

A banging came from the other side of the wall, disgruntled neighbours. Neddy banged back. 'Mind your own business! Or I will burn your fucking house down!'

I backed out of the room and out of the house. No one made any qualms.

Shouting from the house continued as I opened my car

door. Cooper was sitting in the driver's seat. He'd done a crap on the passenger's seat. The car reeked.

I exclaimed something and scared him. He turned and dove into the passenger footwell. I felt awful and got in the car, making gentle soothing sounds and patting the top of his head. 'It's okay, boy. No one's going to hurt you now.'

15

I got home, threw some kibble around the flat to keep Cooper busy, then went back to the car to deal with his mess. I came back inside and sat down, frustrated that an hour had passed since I'd arrived home, and I'd been dealing with dog admin all that time. Then I thought, at least the dog was a sentient being, whereas, for the rest of the day, I was following a case that no one had any interest in me getting to the bottom of.

He needed a walk. That he hadn't had a walk all day was probably the reason he'd made a mess in the car. I sighed, got up and grabbed the lead. Cooper wagged his tail.

I took him on a long walk, guilty about the lack of exercise he'd had with me. Maybe soiling the car was an act of revenge. Then it occurred to me we were on his old street when it happened. A little dog trauma perhaps?

We walked through Bishops Avenue, towards Hampstead Heath, around Kenwood and back down North Hill. I was sure I'd knacker us both out and we'd arrive home to sleep the sleep of the righteous.

Of course, the case and all its players rolled around in my head. I was done with it, I decided.

Done with it.

I had to talk to William Donsaw. He was the last player I hadn't spoken to. I'd seek him out and have a talk with him. Then that would be it. I would be done with it. Maybe.

Back inside, I checked my phone and saw a message from Kim. *How's it going?* Was she referring to my first day as a dog owner, or that a femme fatale had laid a wet one on me last night and I was still trying to work out what it could mean? I delayed replying.

I got into bed and, after an hour, realised I wasn't going to sleep anytime soon. I turned on my lamp and that got Cooper excited. I tussled with him on the floor a bit. After a few minutes, I'd stop and he'd look at me, like he was asking, 'What's next?' Was I supposed to be constantly walking or playing with him?

I dug out the Poirot mystery I'd started reading in Keany's cafe. Cooper looked on, so I got up and brought his bed into the room, and he lay in it. Every once in a while, he'd get excited and do a dance, coming close and moving away when I'd reach out.

Hours passed. Detective Poirot got his man. I dozed and awoke a little while before dawn. I made a kibble hunt for Cooper and headed out.

I'd seen from my previous visit it was forbidden to park on Fitzroy Park, unless I was a resident. But there was plenty of space, and I parked, ready to swallow up the cost of a ticket.

The early hours of the morning passed. Just me and the smell Cooper had left in the car. I had the window open despite the morning chill.

An old Stones cassette played in the tape deck. Yes,

Merkel was old enough to have one of those, though I don't think of her as an old car. She'd managed to keep a kind of new sheen and had never given me too many problems.

I supposed the Donsaw boys awoke and spent the day at their clubs. That was why the house was such a mess, Edward Donsaw left to fend for himself each day. They appeased him by bringing home a bottle of booze on their return.

That Robert returned home before William the previous day left me hopeful they would leave separately again.

A black Mercedes arrived. The driver got out and opened the gates. Then he got back in the car and drove inside. Within a moment, he was on his way out with Robert Donsaw in the backseat. It was 9am. He must have been the earlier riser.

AN HOUR LATER, an identical model of car arrived for the other brother, and William Donsaw appeared. He looked older than Robert, carried more weight and wasn't as tall — under six foot; balding, with a narrow tent of hair on top of his head. His hair and eyebrows were white. He had a ruddier complexion than his brother. He wore frameless glasses, a brown suit, which looked matted or suede from a distance, and a brown-and-red striped tie.

The car turned towards the main road. I waited a moment then started after them. They led me into the city and into Mayfair. The car stopped outside one of the many grand grubby French Renaissance buildings on St James's Street. William Donsaw was getting out of the car as I passed, looking to turn off and onto a side street to park.

Shortly thereafter, I walked through an impressive entranceway to a reception desk. Behind the desk was a young man, who looked fresh out of a prestigious University, and an elder statesman. They both acknowledged me. The attention of the senior receptionist lingered with me.

I wasn't wearing a suit but was dressed smartly enough not to feel self-conscious. Proper shoes, jeans black enough they could be trousers, and a thick-knit jumper under a smart jacket — a young entrepreneur who didn't need to flaunt it. I said in my most refined voice I was a friend of William Donsaw and wanted to drop in on him. He wasn't expecting me, I said, but my name was Mike Seferis, and I had a message I wanted to relay to him in person.

The senior receptionist looked me over. I didn't flinch. He made a call, and I imagined an old-fashioned telephone being brought to William's table. I was told, 'You're welcome to see him, sir. He's having breakfast in the main dining room, two flights up and to the left.'

I walked up a marble staircase and entered a grand dining room, with columns coming down from the ceiling like an old Viennese coffee house. There was a scatter of men having breakfast and coffee. I scanned the room for William Donsaw. I wasn't expecting him to come and introduce himself. I wasn't sure what I'd expected. When I saw him, he looked up and back down at the plate he was working on.

'Mr Donsaw,' I said. 'Mike Seferis.'

He nodded.

'May I take a seat?'

He continued to nod, more absent-mindedly than enthusiastically. He had a piece of toast in one hand and the paper in the other. Before him was a neatly arranged English breakfast, heavy on the meat, a cup of coffee and a tall glass of champagne. Despite the decadent feast before him, his face was miserable. His cheeks were unshaven, the hair he did have was messy and in need of a trim. His tie was loose.

A waiter appeared with a silver pot and topped up William's coffee cup. He placed a cup and saucer in front of me and waited for me to nod. I nodded.

A miniature milk jug was on the table. I reached for it and asked, 'May I?'

William nodded without looking up, painfully shy.

I poured a splash. The coffee was heavy, oily and sour. I resisted a grimace as I felt it sliding into my gut. Now and then, William would look up at me, then lower his eyes again.

'I don't know if your brother told you about me,' I said. 'I'm a private investigator. A few days ago, your father, as sharp and charming as could be, came to my office and asked me to help a young man called Neddy Mara.'

William eyed me again. His expression was less vacant. I couldn't say what replaced it, but I at least felt reassured that someone was there and a carer wasn't about to join us and ask what I was doing.

'Your father said Neddy was a friend of the family, but it turns out he might be the boy's grandfather. He's been bankrolling him since he was a teenager. I went to your house yesterday to ask him some questions and found him in an incoherent state. That's when I met Robert.'

I was choosing my words carefully, and I didn't want to tell him I'd seen Amaryllis. He seemed fragile, like a man who could just about manage his daily routine; I was guessing this was the reason Robert had asked me to leave him alone.

'What's Neddy like?' William asked, his voice quiet and child-like.

'Volatile,' I said. 'Aggressive.'

William kept his gaze on me, the kind of gaze that makes a person want to continue speaking, but I didn't want to expand on what I'd said.

He cut into a banger and chewed, expressionless. Then he said, 'He was brought up by a gangster. What do you expect?'

'Derek O'Mara,' I said. Fearful eyes flicked up at me before returning downward. 'I spoke to him. He said he was terrified of your father.'

I waited for a reaction, received none, and prodded further. 'Why would a gangster, as you call him, be terrified of your father?'

William wasn't thrown by the question. Without putting his cutlery down, he said, 'You'd be right to fear the entitled nobility. They're capable of anything.'

I waited for him to speak further and took a sip of oily coffee, tepid now.

'What does the boy look like?' William asked.

I skipped Neddy's personal style choices. 'Dark hair, dark eyes, thin lipped, broad forehead. I see him in your father's face.' I didn't say that only happened when his father was being a raging drunk. 'I see him in *your* face.'

The waiter returned and topped up our coffee cups. I sat back and took in the interaction between servant and upper cruster. Beyond them were maroon walls and drapes that made the room feel like a womb. Surrounding us were portraits of esteemed men, one sitting at a desk in thinker pose, another standing in a long, bohemian robe, but mostly basic portraits of stern faces giving us sidelong glances.

I said, 'You're Neddy's father, aren't you?'

He'd been cutting into a slice of black pudding. His knife paused for a moment, then he continued to eat.

'I suppose it was all very scandalous. Your father made threats, and Catherine went to Derek O'Mara to feel safe.'

William made no confirmation or correction.

'You know she died? She took her own life a year ago.'

He ceased eating again. He didn't take his eyes from his plate. Then he dropped his cutlery and covered his face, his shoulders quaking. He was silently sobbing.

Shit. I'd broken him. I looked around, self-conscious. A man with a full beard at the nearest table was tucking into a steak. Two men at the next table were nursing their coffees. No one looked over.

I gave him some time. 'I'm sorry, William.'

He recovered and took a deep breath. 'She was a goddess. No man, at least no man as weak as myself, could resist her. As for her part, I suspect it was a form of revenge. This moneyed family had rejected her, so by spending time with me, she created a rift.'

This was the secret that had poisoned the family. Catherine had been rejected by Robert. So she went to William to conceive a child and then took the baby to Derek, where the Donsaws couldn't touch her.

Sure, I thought, two brothers spend all their days in members clubs in Mayfair but different ones. I couldn't imagine they were modern enough men to talk about feelings and find it within themselves to bury the hatchet. I *could* imagine a lifetime of repressed emotions and simmering tension.

However, Donsaw senior approached the wayward teenager and corrupted him with money, taking away any hope Catherine had of getting the boy under control. Maybe he told a few evils in the boy's ear. If the boy hated his mother the way he seemed to hate everything else in the world, I could see that driving a woman to take her own life. And the vicious cycle of hatred was complete.

Perhaps hiring me was Donsaw's need to look out for Neddy, an attempt to do some good. But it was too little too late. After a life of poisoning the air and instilling fear in those around him, he'd lost his mind.

'But you and your brother still live under the same roof,' I said.

'I spend most of my time here,' William said. 'I often stay. They have comfortable rooms upstairs. Though I do need to bring my father something to eat now and then. He needs something to sustain him.'

I took a few more sips of coffee in case he had anything more to say, then I thanked William Donsaw for his time and left.

Bring my father something to eat now and then. I marvelled at the callousness, but then, the Donsaws amazed me every time I met one of them.

16

I got caught in traffic on the way home and started feeling anxious about Cooper — jeez, my life really wasn't my own anymore.

I got there and could hear Cooper's whining from the hallway. By the time I ascended the stairs, eager to end his misery, Joel appeared in the doorway.

'Got yourself a dog, or is that a mourning widow locked in your place?'

'Hi, Joel. It's a dog.'

'Got it for Christmas, did you?'

'Something like that,' I said, eager to get inside and stop the whining.

'You never struck me as a dog person.'

'Joel, I'm sorry if the noise was disturbing you.'

'Crikey, it wasn't disturbing me, it just made me curious.'

'Well, now you have the answer to the riddle.'

'You're making it sound like I'm a busybody. He's been crying all day above my shop, yesterday too.'

'It's not been all day, and OK, the noise disturbed you. You could have just said.'

The Highgate Murder

'It's not the noise, *Mike*. It's the cruelty.'

I was taken aback for a moment, regrouped and said, 'Who's being cruel?'

'Let me just think over my sentence. Oh yes. You.'

'Are you serious?'

'No, I'm a comedian practising material.'

'Don't give up your day job being a grumpy old arsehole. It suits you better.'

'Thanks. At least it suits me. You're acting like one thirty years ahead of schedule.'

'Sorry if my timing's off. I guess I didn't organise my life plan as well as you.'

'OK, nice to know where I stand. Since you moved in, I sensed you had a problem with me. I'd have thought giving you an apartment full of cheap antique furniture, and dragging you home, raving, from the pub, would have scored me some points.'

'I didn't ask you to do that, Saint Joel. Do you know how exhausting it is having a neighbour who needs everyone to like him, so he can be Postman Pat, driving around, having everyone in his neighbourhood wave at him? Sorry if I don't feel like joining the club.'

'Do you have a problem with me because I'm a grumpy old arsehole or because I'm a friendly old fruit?'

'Give it a rest, Joel. I know your true colours.'

'What true colours?'

'Forget it.'

'No. What? Have I *ever* been unneighbourly? Ever not given you a warm hello?'

'Not since I've been old enough to talk back.'

'Eh? What are you talking about?'

'OK. You used to call our home when I was a kid, because some appliance in your flat wasn't working. If my father wasn't home and I had to answer; if you couldn't get your needs met in that instant, you'd go off at me, effing and blinding like a psycho. I was a kid. You used to scare the crap out of me.'

'I never did that.'

'Oh OK. Sorry, I'm making it up.'

'When was this? If you were answering your father's phone, you must be talking about twenty... twenty-five or something years ago?'

'So?'

'How many times did it happen?'

'What does that matter?'

'If I did, I'm sorry.'

'You're just sorry I know the real you, no matter how much you act like a friendly old fruit.'

'I have no memory of effing and blinding at you.'

'I guess you were too drunk.'

'Maybe I was. Maybe it was when I had cancer, or when my partner was in the hospital, dying, and maybe I went off at you because I saw you as the curt little brat son of my landlord who I couldn't afford to pay rent to and I was being an arsehole. It was over twenty years ago!'

'I know it was! I'm not even arguing about that. This is about right now, you minding your own business!'

'Oh! Right. God forbid anyone poke their nose into the important business of the cool loner in his leather jacket, who doesn't need anyone and wants to deny he lives in a building with other people. Only it's your neighbour, who you can barely bring yourself to say good morning to, who's carrying you home every night.'

'That happened twice!'

'And how many times did I verbally abuse you on the phone?'

Once was the answer; I felt it was too superfluous a point to mention, but it showed he remembered.

'You can't even ask someone to dog-sit while you're out all morning so me and my customers get to hear a crying mutt all day. And what else isn't my business? Oh yes. You walk around all day like you have a pole up your arse, then later in the day you get smashed in the pub across the street and everything you hold in comes firing out, so everyone nearby has to run for cover. And muggins here has to vouch for you and carry you home when you're left flat at the end of it. If your old man could see you now.'

'You didn't know my father. He collected your rent.'

'Yeah, for thirty years. You're right, hardly knew the man at all.'

Cooper had been whining all this time. He could hear our voices and was near the door. I finally opened it and he came bursting out.

He raced halfway down the stairs, then up again, jumped up to put his two front paws on my leg, jumped off, and danced on the small landing like a fly trapped in a glass. When he saw Joel, he half ran, half tumbled down the stairs and danced there.

Joel laughed. 'Cute little bugger, deserves more than to be locked inside all day.'

'Plenty of people leave their pets at home during the workday.'

'Plenty of people throw shopping trolleys into Regent's canal.'

'I do that too.'

'I bet you do.'

Cooper had diffused the tension. We were bantering now. 'Cooper's a rescue,' I said. 'His previous owner beat him and I got him... confiscated... or whatever the word is. I mean, not on purpose. Look, I've got lumbered with him after I unintentionally reported him.' A thought occurred to me; it broke my heart a little, but it made perfect sense. 'Do you want him?'

'What?'

'You like the *little bugger*.'

'I can't just take on a dog.'

'Welcome to my world. Careful what you complain about. You might end up becoming a dog owner.'

'You could have refused him.'

'Do you think I didn't try?'

'I'm sure you did.'

Joel tried to ruffle Cooper's hair, but Cooper expertly dodged him. Now he was running up and down the stairs in excitement.

'Let's take him to the pub and have a drink,' Joel said.

'The pub? I wouldn't know how to keep him still, and I don't know if he's house-trained, or pub-trained.'

'That's why we're going. I used to have a dog. I can show you a few tricks.'

I couldn't think of a decent excuse why not, and after the exchange we'd just had, our relationship would be very strained if I refused. I stuffed my pockets with dog paraphernalia and attached the lead to Cooper's collar.

We all walked out the front door together and Cooper immediately strained against the lead, trying to devour every bit of garbage on the street, crusts of a sandwich, a dirty tissue, the shit of other dogs.

'You're going to strangle him that way,' Joel said, helpfully.

'What should I do? Let him chase cars?'

Joel turned left and walked in the opposite direction of The Woodman. 'Follow me.'

On the corner of Archway Road and Southwood Lane was a pet shop, its pet shop smell almost overwhelming. Joel asked what treats I had on me. I dipped into my pocket and showed him — a handful of kibble. He picked out a bag of dried pepperoni slices. He also bought a harness. Well, he didn't buy it. I forked the money over.

He led us to the woods. When we were a safe distance inside, away from the exit and the road, he showed Cooper we had the treats. He released the lead, then gave him a treat, and Cooper scarpered off. My heart skipped a beat. 'Joel, if that dog gets himself killed—'

'Stop imagining the worst-case scenario. Food is his primal instinct. He doesn't care about anything else. He's had his balls cut off.'

'What?'

'Didn't you know?'

'How the hell would I know that?'

'Because he doesn't have any.'

'I wasn't looking that closely at his balls, or... where his balls are supposed to be. Anyway, he's covered in hair.'

'—and by the way he pees. He doesn't lift one leg in the air.'

Indeed, Cooper squatted to pee. 'Oh.'

We walked along behind the poor dog. Joel called out to him, waving the bag of treats in the air. Cooper came back for a treat, then rushed off again. We repeated the process.

Cooper ran elegantly, a natural athlete in his element in the woods. He bounded about as if he knew the place intimately, alternately sprinting around in the distance and trotting alongside us as we walked a circuit.

Ominous clouds appeared, then a gushing summer rain began. We gathered Cooper and legged it to The Woodman. Joel led us to a table. I offered to get drinks, but he said they looked after him there. We sat down, with Cooper by our feet — staring into space. Joel showered affection on him, asking him who's a good boy, trying to ruffle his ears. Without moving away, Cooper shifted and squirmed so Joel couldn't quite get a hand on him.

Rachel approached and bantered with Joel. She asked what we'd have to drink.

'Two pints of London,' Joel said. It would be my first drink since the insanity in Soho. The thought made me panic, but having not eaten all day, the heaviness of a beer was appealing.

Rachel brought the drinks and I all but downed mine. Joel didn't raise an eyebrow.

'Sorry I let off in the hallway,' I said.

'I didn't smell anything.'

'I meant emotionally. I already had guilt issues over the dog. Any other day I might have looked into doing something about him, but... I'm really getting deep into a case.'

'A case?'

'Yeah.'

'What do you do?'

'I'm a private investigator.'

'Fuck off.'

I stayed where I was.

'*What?*'

'What?'

He clarified, 'A private investigator? Like Columbo?'

'Well... sure.'

'You're telling me all that talk in here the other night about "working a case" was for real?'

'Oh man. What did I say?'

'I thought it was the plot of the latest mystery you were reading.'

'I hope everyone else listening assumed that. Did I mention any names?'

'It sounded more like gibberish than anything else. I always wondered who those people were, going into your place. I thought you were a therapist, or a financial adviser.'

'A financial adviser?'

My glass was empty. Joel waved to Rachel as she passed. 'Get this man another beer.'

'I better not.'

'Don't worry. I'll keep an eye on you,' he said, and he chuckled.

'What's so funny?'

'When you were a kid, your father used to bring you into the bookshop and you'd buy all the cheap mystery novels, all the old, green Penguin books. You were allowed to buy one each time you came in.'

I nodded. 'Yeah, I remember. I still have them all.'

'I still have *boxes* of those old mysteries in storage. I had to shift my stock when I had to start selling furniture instead of books. You want them?'

'*Yes.*'

'We can drive down one day to the storage unit, pile them in and bring them over to your place, if you have the space.'

'Do you want any money for them?'

'Nah. They're costing me in storage. I should get rid of the other books too, but that would be admitting I'll never be a bookseller again. I warn you, there's a lot of them.'

'Great.'

'Where will you put them?'

'In the flat. I just pile them high. If I get them up to the ceiling, it'll save me ever having to paint the walls.'

'Sounds cluttered.'

'It's a bachelor pad. I'm a bachelor. A pile of green Penguins is all I need.'

For those who don't get that reference, the earliest Penguin books were colour coded. Fiction was orange, crime fiction was green. I think travel was blue and biography was purple.

'Sounds to me like the perfect time to become a dog owner,' Joel said.

I opened my mouth to argue, but, dang, he had me there.

'When you're going out for a long while, you can bring him to the shop. He can keep me company. If we're not around when you get back, we'll most likely be in the woods, or here.'

'This neighbourhood suits you, eh?'

Joel nodded. 'It's quiet, it's green, a stone's throw from London proper, a good place to be melancholy, a good place to be creative.'

'Creative? How do you get creative?'

'I write a little poetry. I don't publish anymore.'

'When did you publish?'

He looked at me, amused. 'Mostly in the sixties, did some work for the National and the RSC, Eric Gregory Award in the seventies.'

'What?' I blurted. I couldn't help it. This cantankerous furniture salesman? Amazing, the assumptions we make about people.

I was embarrassed at my ignorance. It was funny; Pap never mentioned it, and yet he talked constantly about his partner, Dan, the musician. 'Sorry, I didn't know.'

'Don't be sorry for not reading outside the detective genre.'

'Hey, I like the classics. Okay, I've never read poetry. I've tried.'

Joel laughed.

'Why did you stop?'

'I didn't stop writing, I publishing. That aspect interested me less. I was happy running my shop.'

He told me his business started as a second-hand furniture shop, but people started dropping off stacks of old books, so he focused on books. He was living his dream. He and Dan hosted music performances and readings, which was surprising to me; his shop had as much floor space as my kitchen. Joel shared his work that way instead of publishing. Some impressive names of the local artistic alumni would partake, quite the cultural hub.

Rachel brought us thick-cut ham sandwiches. And fresh pints. Joel would just make a signal and she would bring them over. They kept coming until I lost count. We drank quickly. I didn't know if I was trying to keep up with him or if he was trying to keep up with me. It was an easy thing to do when you didn't have to walk to the bar.

Joel told me about his life as I prodded him with questions. Dan died ten years ago and Joel didn't keep up the social aspect of the shop. Then a few years ago it stopped turning a profit, and he put the books in storage and went back to selling furniture.

'It wouldn't have turned a profit at all if your father wasn't renting to us dirt cheap,' he said. 'I think he had a soft spot for Dan, the horn-player.'

'Dad liked his jazz.'

'Then a couple of years ago, he offered to sell me the place. Asked me what I could afford, which wasn't much, and I paid him in sporadic instalments. Now I'm financially secure, thanks to him. *Lovely* bloke. He came to see us in the hospital when Dan was ill. I thought it was because we were behind on rent, but he paid Dan's hospital bills.'

I didn't respond. Adrenaline was surging through me as aspects of my life Joel wasn't aware of fell into place.

Unawares, Joel took a drink. 'I was sorry when he passed away.'

Silence ensued. We did some drinking. Cooper had gone to sleep under the table. Summer rain pounded at the windows.

'Something wrong?' Joel asked.

Thoughts were flying around in my head. If I opened my mouth to start voicing them... I didn't know where it would go.

I opened my mouth. 'He sold you your flat cheap because he wanted to get his hands on quick cash.'

Joel crinkled his eyebrows into a question mark. 'Oh?'

'We had a gambler in the family. My wife's brother, Paul. First time he stayed with us, he left with Alison's life savings. Second time he appeared, he had a debt ten times the size of his previous one and, so he said, his life had been threatened. Before Alison could get her mind around what he'd told her, he disappeared, but called her shortly thereafter to tell her everything was fine.'

Joel was right there with me. 'Nick gave him the money.'

'According to you, that's exactly when he sold the flat. I can imagine what he got from you was the amount Paul needed. It was *good-old-Nick*, giving the tout a tenner behind Steve's back.'

'What?'

'Nothing,' I said. I felt tears behind my eyes. Pap had played a role in the Incident. I hated him in that moment. 'Why couldn't he have kept his big nose out of it?' I asked.

'He knew he was on his way out,' Joel said. 'That's the

ultimate time for good deeds. He didn't just see it as helping your wife's brother, or getting him off your back, but it saved my bacon too.'

'I wish he hadn't.'

'Thanks.'

'No, I mean, if he hadn't enabled that addict, things would have been different. If one element of Paul's scheming life had been different, things wouldn't have worked out the way they did.'

Joel tapped the side of his glass with his fingernails, coming up with different rhythms. 'Now I know why he told me never to tell you. I guess the gambling brother-in-law was a strain on your marriage?'

I couldn't even respond to that, the biggest understatement I'd ever heard.

'Is that the reason you separated?'

I looked up at him, confused. I thought he'd known.

'You still wear your wedding ring.'

'I'm a widower,' I said.

Joel looked at me blankly.

'She was murdered.'

17

I watched Joel's face as he absorbed the fact, blank to confusion to shock.

It wasn't something I voluntarily told people, but I was liquored up, and still reeling from the news that Pap had given up one of his properties, achieving nothing in the process except delaying the inevitable tragedy.

Cooper sat up and rested his chin on my leg. I patted his head, then gave him a stroke and ruffled his ears and chest. It was the first time he'd allowed such contact. Did he have a sixth sense for things like this?

I can't say why I laid it all out for Joel. Maybe this realisation about Pap took me back to the Incident, and I couldn't go through it all again, not on my own.

'What happened next time the brother appeared?' Joel asked.

'He gambled up a new debt, ten times the size of the one my father bailed him out of. His life was on the line again. A gambling friend of his had dirt on a gangster he was working for — er... we'll call him Barry. Barry was in the drug game, and was involved in all the murder and police corrupting that went along with it. This evidence exposed all of that.

'The friend let Paul know the whereabouts of this evidence before getting himself bumped off for knowing too much. Paul saw this as a blackmail opportunity that would save his life. He made contact with Barry, and they agreed a price and an exchange location. Paul said he was getting an ignorant, innocent bag man to make the exchange. That was a lie. The truth was, he was planning to push his own sister into being the intermediary.

'He told Alison what he wanted her to do and she agreed to go along with it. If I'd have known what she was doing, I'd have told her it was suicide. Maybe she knew that. Maybe she saw her brother as her responsibility and blamed herself for how things turned out.

'They were amateurs dealing with pros. As soon as Paul placed the call to Barry, they had a private detective looking for him. *What people could get their hands on that information? And who did those people spend their time with? And who of those people had astronomical, illegal gambling debts?*

'They worked out who Paul was, but they couldn't find him. Alison didn't know how stacked the deck was against her. She walked into a lion's den. They beat her and killed her, possibly trying to get an angle on Paul's whereabouts, or because the man whose job it was to deal with her was a psychopath who liked to beat and kill people.'

'Jesus.'

'I had to identify the body. I received a letter from her a day later. She'd addressed it to herself. See, if everything would have turned out okay, I wouldn't have touched it, and she could have thrown it away. But she was dead. I opened it. She said goodbye, told me what she was doing, making an exchange for Paul for some scam he had going. She knew it was dangerous. *He told them I have nothing to do with this. I'm just a nobody, getting a fee for delivering a message. He figures they'll look kindlier on a woman. I know you'll never understand, but he's my little brother. Dad died when I was fourteen and he was six.* She'd spelt fourteen wrong, without a u.'

'I DON'T KNOW how you made it through,' Joel said.

'Working for the Met wasn't going to work for me. Watching CCTV footage for a living was too much time to think. I became a private detective. I keep busy, and next on my agenda is figuring out who set fire to Neddy Mara's roof terrace.'

Joel nodded. 'And you're in it pretty deep, you were saying.'

'Uh huh.'

Joel continued to nod his head. Then he stopped. 'Who's Neddy Mara?'

Joel was the only person in my life now who didn't know the ins and outs of the case, and he probably did know most of it due to my drunken blabbering. And I think I needed to tell a new narrative, get the taste of the story I'd just told out of my mouth.

I started at the beginning. I didn't mention Donsaw by name, but when I said I'd been told to keep my payment in the understanding that I stop working on the case, Joel enquired into the size of the payment. I told him. He whistled.

'They can afford it,' I said. 'He lives in one of those massive houses on the Heath.'

'Where?'

Maybe it was the beer. I told him.

'The Donsaw house,' he stated.

'How did you know that?'

'I know all about that family.'

'Really?'

'Sure. I know about all the strange, reclusive characters in our neighbourhood.'

'Like what?'

'They're an old-money family in one of the most expensive houses in London. They've owned that house for at least sixty years. And the ones who are no longer with us are all interred in an elegant mausoleum in Highgate Cemetery.'

'How could you know all that?'

'I know that last bit because I'm a Friend of Highgate Cemetery.'

'A friend of the cemetery?'

'Yes.'

'What does that mean?'

'I volunteer there.'

'Are they promising you a good rate when your time comes or something?'

'It's an important part of the community and Highgate's heritage.'

'OK.'

'It's not morbid.'

'OK.'

'People come from all over the world to see that place. They do walking tours in there.'

'Walking tours? Like seeing celebrity houses in Hollywood, but... celebrity graves?'

'There are architectural treasures there, stories...'

'What kind of stories?'

Joel lifted his head, as if for inspiration. He gestured with his finger. 'See these paintings?'

I nodded. Lots of familiar prints of pretty women, reclining in loose, brightly coloured clothing that dripped off them like caramel. I'd not noticed them before.

'These are all by the Pre-Raphaelites, the romantics of the Victorian era. Things were all a bit grey and religious in those days and this was the reaction. They wrote passionate love poetry—'

'And painted hot redheads,' I said.

'Quite. They're all interred in the cemetery. So, here's a story you couldn't make up. You see the young lady in this picture.' He pointed to a young woman floating on her back in a river. 'The model in that painting is Lizzie Siddal. She was a muse of the Pre-Raphaelite Brotherhood and an artist in her own right, and she was the lover of Rossetti, one of the founders of the Brotherhood.

'She died of an opium overdose. Rossetti was heartbroken and wrote love poems that he placed in her coffin. A few years later, he wondered what possessed him to bury perfectly good poetry and ordered the coffin to be exhumed. He took back his poetry and published it... You okay?'

I'd been staring at the painting of the woman in the river. The story whirled in my head. 'I want to go there.'

'You want to do a tour of the *celebrity graves*?'

'I need to go there. Now.'

'So you're a crazy drunk.'

'You got a key, right? You have to get me into the Donsaw mausoleum. There's something I need to see.'

'You're serious?'

'Joel, I need to go there. Now. I need to see the place. You can get me in there.'

'Right. Except I don't have authority to do spontaneous

tours there, in the middle of the night, in pouring rain, for my Brahms-and-Liszt neighbour.'

'You know why I do this weird job. You know what drives me. I have to get to the bottom of this, and I know the answer's in there.'

18

We'd been drinking in the pub the entire day. Outside it was dark and raining. Joel went to the bar and asked Rachel for a couple of umbrellas. She reached down and plucked a couple of massive black ones with curved handles. I looked at Joel quizzically. He explained, 'So many people forget their brollies here, they have an endless supply under the bar.'

The short walk up the steep hill to Highgate village took about twenty minutes. Cooper wasn't straining against the lead too badly, happy to shelter beneath our brollies.

We walked through the village and down Swains lane, a narrow street that ran parallel to the cemetery, protected by a ten-foot wall.

We approached the entrance, a building that looked like a miniature Gothic Tudor castle, its yellow bricks blackened with time. At its centre was a large grill gate, with the open cemetery on the other side.

Joel couldn't repress the tour guide in him. 'Before London's population boom a couple of centuries ago, people were buried in churchyards. In the 1800s, commercial cemeteries were created. This is one of the Magnificent Seven.' He listed off the other six.

My quirkiness may have demanded we come here but it was his that made him assent to the idea. He'd probably been waiting years for a crazy neighbour to demand he be brought here surreptitiously, in the dead of night — his access and knowledge essential to the cause.

Joel took a set of old-fashioned keys out of inside blazer pocket. He handed me a pocket torch to shine on the lock for him. I resisted calling him a boy scout. He opened the gate and we entered into Highgate Cemetery.

Joel explained the room to our left was the chapel. To our right was an office he let himself into. I hung by the door. If Cooper was to go in and shake off his wet fur, it would have left a rather conspicuous mess. 'There are master keys for each section,' Joel said. 'Anglican, Baptists, dissenters...' He held up a key. 'This will get us into the Donsaw mausoleum.'

He locked the door behind him and we entered the cemetery proper.

The smell of damp earth in our nostrils, we walked along a rocky path, our shoes squishing on mud and leaves. I'd been picturing us walking around with a torch or an old-fashioned lamp, but the grounds were surprisingly well lit by the dappled moonlight that reached us through the branches of trees. Tilting gravestones reflected the light. Stone lions and dogs stood vigil at some of them. Angels guarded others and lay in repose on others. Broken columns symbolised lives cut short, empty chairs symbolised a missing sitter, and urns with a cloth covering them symbolised something else. A lot of monuments had turned bright green with moss, some were obscured with ivy.

Murders of crows looked upon us from tall trees that

sheltered us from the rain. The trees grew around and sometimes through the graves and gravestones, lifting and breaking them, creating a decorative fusion of wood and stone, along with a chaotic tangle of sprawling tree roots, bushes, tall grass and wild-flowers. It was hard to see where anything started and ended. I allowed Cooper to hold us back a little for some sniffs. It was the least we owed him.

'We call it managed neglect,' Joel said. 'Curbing nature to an extent but allowing it to thrive and dominate the man-made aspect. There's a Gothic beauty to it, or call it an excuse, we can't find enough volunteers to keep everything maintained.'

'Joel,' I said. 'What is that?'

A creature stood in front of us, its yellow eyes staring.

'Fox,' Joel said.

Obvious, once you knew the answer. They let out intermittent howls. The cold made my body want to shiver; I let my limbs hang loose so as not to. I made affirmative sounds and words to compliment Joel's spiels. He pointed out some famous painters, writers, actors and old TV personalities.

He explained we were passing through Egyptian Avenue. I wondered if this was the direct route, or if he was taking a detour to show me the dramatic architecture. 'The more money you were willing to spend, the fancier your environment could be,' he said. 'Two centuries ago the idea of Egypt was very popular.'

It really felt like another world. We passed under a Gothic stone archway with Egyptian-style columns, dripping with ivy. The stone-walled avenue had black doorways, each containing a vault for the dead. Some vaults had grill gates, I could see through to a grid system where the dead were stacked. Names were inscribed on square slabs of marble. Some had dates, some had words of love, like:

We'll meet again. I noticed one that read: *Alison, Love You Forever.*

'The Donsaw mausoleum is just ahead,' Joel said. I followed his silhouette and we approached a tomb. At the top, between two carved wreaths, was the family name.

Joel unlocked heavy double doors, thick with cobwebs, with a chunky key. We entered and descended steep steps. A striking stain-glass window of autumnal colours provided enough light.

At the bottom of the stairs was an elaborate mosaic floor, with a drain at the centre for the rain water. Shelves of old, damp, dark-wood coffins with Gothic steel handles surrounded us.

'What the shit!' I hissed. By my ear I noticed at least two of the biggest spiders I'd ever seen, with bodies like black eggs.

'They're meta bournetis, harmless and very rare,' Joel said proudly. 'The wildlife trust were very excited to find them here.'

'Guess I got excited too. Can I borrow your torch?'

I studied some of the names and dates on the coffins, Francis Owen Nield Donsaw 1872-1931. Right Honourable Herbert McMullan Donsaw, 1862-1932, Louisa Andre Donsaw 1914-2002, General Arnold Douglas Donsaw 1926-2007.

Joel was talking in the background. 'A lot of these places were damaged when the cemetery was in disrepair, before the Friends took over in the seventies. We had specialists come in to do things like lovingly repair stain-glass windows that were smashed and masonry that was damaged...'

'What's up there?' I asked, pointing to a small coffin just below the ceiling, almost out of sight.

'Too sad for me to guess,' Joel said. 'Likely a child. The

curve of the arch means that only a smaller coffin would be able to fit in the space.'

'Why's there no inscription?'

'Maybe there is one, but I can't pull it out for a closer look. It's damp here and the wood rots. It could fall apart.'

'Yes, OK. I'm not asking you to pull it out. If I could get up there and shine the torch into the crannies...'

'Are you asking for a leg up?'

'I don't think so. Imagine us having to get an ambulance down here once you crash under my weight.'

'You think I can't lift you up there?'

'Not really, no.'

'I beg to differ.'

His machismo was amusing, but I wanted a closer look at the small coffin. 'Alright, let's do it. Ready?'

It was awkward. He cupped his hands for my foot. I stepped into the stirrup and launched myself upward, my hand on the wall for balance. I shone the torch at the small rotting coffin. There was no name or marking. Plenty more meta bourneti spiders, though. I felt like Indiana Jones.

I could feel Joel shaking under me.

'On three,' I said. 'You let go, take a step back, and I'll land.'

'Alright,' he huffed through gritted teeth.

I lifted myself on a wall edge for leverage. Joel let go and stepped out of the way. I landed gently enough and no coffin was crashed into.

'Thanks for that,' I said.

'Anytime,' Joel said, trying to control his breathing, like it hadn't been an ordeal.

I took out my notebook and copied down every name and date on every coffin. And every number — Joel explained that each grave (and mausoleum) had a number which made it locatable.

'I want to look through the records,' I said. 'I want to see that small coffin accounted for.

Joel sighed with a determined expression that said he would see this mad plan through to the end. 'OK, let's go.'

We returned to the office, wet and tired. We all entered this time, less caring about getting paw prints on the floor. We left the main light off. Joel didn't want the place to look unnecessarily conspicuous. The moonlight provided some illumination and he used his torch too.

Cooper strained at the lead and I allowed him enough slack to explore every cranny of the office.

'The record of every single burial is kept here,' Joel said, pointing to rows of old tomes lining one of the walls. 'A lot in old logbooks, in beautiful, quite illegible Victorian calligraphy. We're inputting all the data onto computers. Might take a few centuries. This place has been going since 1839.'

We found the Donsaw family on the system, and in the original ledger, and almost every name and number in my notebook was accounted for. There was no mention of the coffin that had been placed high in the small nook.

'Did you get what you wanted?' Joel asked.

I nodded. I must have seemed pretty short on gratitude. I'd closed up, locked up tight where the truth I'd learned couldn't get at me.

19

We walked home in silence and parted at our front door. I thanked him.

'Sure,' Joel said. He was hungover, worn out and wet.

Upstairs, I found a bottle of Bell's left over from the poker game and I drank. Surprise, surprise, it wasn't a happy drunk. I guess I wanted to escape.

I went to the bathroom and took the small bottle of pills from the cupboard, and I lay on the sofa in wet clothes. I dozed and had a lucid dream that I went back to the cemetery. There was no shelter and the rain drenched me through. I came to a grave, no name on the mossy headstone. I burned to know what was beneath the wet earth. I had no shovel. I got down on my knees and dug at the earth with my hands. I knew who it would be, but in the strange way of dreams, my knowledge changed, my father, Alison, Catherine Moore, a child. I felt myself merge into the black earth as I awoke in the darkness of my empty home, the sound of cars revving and swooshing on the Archway road outside my window.

I threw a handful of kibble around for Cooper and headed out. My head was fuzzy and I told myself this was real, the way we tell ourselves in dreams that this must be real, despite our doubts. The car smelled of dog-shit, that was real enough. This couldn't be a dream.

I drove to Edward Donsaw's house, parked illegally and walked through the unlocked gate. The front door was closed this time. I pressed the intercom.

It was late morning. The sons would be out having their champagne breakfasts by now.

'What?' barked a voice.

'Mr Donsaw, it's Mike Seferis.'

There was a pause, then the door buzzed open.

I headed straight to where I expected to find him. He was in his armchair with a whisky bottle by his side and a half full glass in his hand, like he'd been suspended in time.

He looked at me and demanded, 'Did you bring my bottle?'

'Bit early, isn't it?' I said. I wasn't sure why I'd said it, and to stop him going off on a tirade, I said, 'This case has had me hitting the booze hard myself. I wouldn't have lasted as long as you if it was something I'd had to live with every day of my life.'

He didn't reply. He only looked at me with his twisted, unhappy expression and vacant eyes.

I pulled up a wooden chair to sit in front of him. Less comfortable than a church pew, it had a straight back-frame that went upward and across, but the frame was hollow, forcing me to sit upright without any back support. I said, 'I've been to the Donsaw mausoleum in Highgate cemetery.'

His expression didn't change, except for the eyes, which finally focused on me with less vacancy. So he was there.

I didn't know what I was doing, but somehow I felt that I

had a part to play, and decided where I would start my story. 'You had a wife, Mr Donsaw, and she left you, for a younger man, a man with no money.'

Donsaw looked away to the side. He brought his drink to his lips, then quietly snickered.

'You couldn't control her,' I said. 'Even with your abundant wealth. Was she anything like Catherine Moore? A fun-loving woman, not of this stuffy world?'

He said nothing.

'Both your sons had women in their lives, women who weren't of this world. You disapproved of them and bullied your boys into rejecting them. One was a mild-mannered musician. She left quietly enough. The other was Catherine Moore, and she had a child with Robert. There was nothing you could do about that. You could stop a marriage, but you couldn't stop them living in sin.'

His eyes were burning now. Perhaps mine were too.

'What happened next, Donsaw? There's a child-sized, unmarked box in your family mausoleum in Highgate cemetery.'

I waited. He didn't speak.

'You put me on a trail that would lead to me finding out your secret. You even blurted the truth out to me. When I was here last, Robert said: *let the past stay buried.* You said: *nice choice of words.*'

Donsaw took a drink, his eyes not leaving mine.

So, he wanted me to go all the way. I said, 'You got your hands on that child, and you snuffed the life out of it. You paid a lot of people off to cover the truth and you put it in an unmarked coffin in a dark corner of the Donsaw mausoleum.'

His lips parted. I braced myself. 'What did she expect?' His voice was a ragged hiss. 'She thought she'd trick her way into this old family? Into this house? Be just like us? Part of us? Cancel out everything we stand for? Everything we've accomplished? Because of one weakness, my weakness, the physical appeal of a woman. It left me open to all this. And my two stupid sons made exactly the same mistake.'

'If you believed that, I don't think you'd have spent the rest of your life going mad in that chair trying to drink yourself to death. And you see your sons every day, reminding you of what you've done. They won't even leave you. That's the tricky thing: when families do abominable things, they're still part of you. You can try to escape them, disobey them, hate them, but it just ends up tearing you up inside. Your sons have given up on life, they live in this big house, in a big mess. They leave you with a bottle for company every morning, stay out all day and maybe come home with just enough food to sustain you. Wouldn't it be easier if they left, made lives for themselves elsewhere, and left you to die?'

'They don't have the balls!' he said, sitting up in his chair, back straight, his glass falling on the floor. It cracked by didn't break into pieces. 'They could have done something. They should have killed me, but just a word to them about not getting a penny from me, and I got away with it. Just like the child. It didn't struggle. It didn't make any noise.' He bent low, his face in his hands, shoulders shaking. He reminded me of William in that moment.

I hadn't truly believed it until now. There could have been some other explanation for what I saw in the cemetery, like a child in the family who died of an illness and a glitch in the records. I felt nauseous to the point of thinking I'd be sick. I reminded myself that detective Nigel Strangeways never leaned over the side of a chair and threw up while hearing a confession. I did what I had to do to keep my physicality in check, I proceeded with the case. 'How did you stop Catherine Moore making a noise?' I said.

Donsaw looked up, breathing hard, his face wet with tears. 'Money,' he said.

I waited.

'Paid a couple of thugs to threaten her,' he went on. 'That was all it took.'

Catherine's fear of what might have been a threat to her life wasn't the same as 'money', but I let it go. I went on with the story. 'But she didn't run away as quickly and quietly as you hoped. She seduced William, bore his child and took it away with her. I don't know if she went to him for comfort and it was an accidental pregnancy, or if it was some way of sticking it to you, or replacing the child you took from her. She went to Derek O'Mara and they could have played happy families.

'But it backfired. Neddy was hateful from the moment he could speak. His parents couldn't control him. Then you approached him in his mid-teens and told him his parents had been lying to him, that he's from a rich family and he's entitled to abundant wealth. I can't imagine how an interaction between you two might have been, but he took your money.

'I don't know if you knew how effective your actions would be. Neddy treated his parents with even more distain. Fun-loving Catherine was worn down by the abuse of her own son and finally she took her own life. Did you know that?'

Glazed eyes gave me no answer or clue. A silence stretched. The room was so quiet, quite a torment in a house with so many tortuous thoughts and ghosts.

'I wasn't trying to corrupt him,' Donsaw eventually said. 'I was giving him an opportunity to get out of the gutter, to make something of himself. I offered him all of this! I thought he had potential.'

'I guess *he* didn't live up to his potential either.'

'You've seen him! He's an animal! There was no chance of having a grandson after a gangster and his whore had done their damage.'

'He didn't fall in line the way you wanted him to,' I said. 'And so we come to your next crime, Mr Donsaw. You found someone who could create and plant a device to start a fire in Neddy's home — you wanted to kill him too — a fire that might well have burned down a house full of flats and killed the innocent people inside it. There are no fire escapes in that old building, so the people in the top floors were especially vulnerable.'

My back was starting to ache. I asked, 'Why couldn't you leave him alone?'

He said nothing. After leaving him ample opportunity, I tried to guess. 'You hate your wife and you don't want your line to continue? Or is it control? You certainly controlled the fate of Catherine Moore. But you can't control Neddy. He is like a wild animal. No threats about cutting off his allowance were going to work with him, so you decided to end him. All I can say is, your attitude and your actions have at least been consistent.

'But here's where your consistency ends. You hire me to follow the trace that leads back to you. And that leaves one last question: Why did you hire me? You told me why each time I've appeared in your house. You want a bottle. You want me to stop you. You've been trying to stop yourself by drinking yourself to death and it hasn't worked. It scares you, how you nearly killed a building full of people. Maybe you're sorry for what you've done.'

I reached into my coat pocket and pulled out my vial of

sleeping pills. 'That's why the fee was so inflated. You were asking me for a special service. Is this the bottle you were referring to?'

The eyes stopped burning. He visibly relaxed. I could see him thinking — it's over, it's out of my hands, an outsider knows the truth now and has chosen to show mercy. He didn't look up at me, but he reached out and took the bottle. He said, 'I'm glad you figured it out, Mr Seferis.' He wrapped his hand around the bottle tightly and closed his eyes. Softly, he said, 'Now get out.'

20

I drove without thinking.

I must have gone through a red light at a junction. A car coming at my side screeched to a halt and thumped its horn. My realisations were as slow as my reactions, and it took a couple of minutes for me to understand how close I'd come to being rammed.

I got to Archway road, parked lazily, illegally, in the first space I saw, and walked up to the flat.

I sat in a chair and stared at the book-wall. I thought, in the immortal words of Kinsey Millhone, I killed a man and it's weighing heavily on my mind.

Other things I have in common with the legendary lady, I'm in my thirties, I'm a PI and I'm alone.

My eyes scan my shelves of crime fiction, books double stacked and piled high, Golden Age to the hard-boiled 70s, Athens-under-the-junta Costas Haritos to original Scandi-crime copper Martin Beck. Some of those beaten up paperbacks I've had since I was a kid.

These walls of books aren't in the office. They'd surely set a few alarm bells ringing if clients came in here to see my primary motivation for doing this job was a lifetime of getting a kick out of mysteries.

Despite life's knocks, I've always been able to sit in a chair, crack open a mystery and lose myself for a while. In this draughty Highgate flat, I read, my pap's old jazz records playing in the background. It helped deal with the chaos of this existence. I had the flat, the music, my books, my work, and that was working for me.

Until now.

There's a big difference between the convenient victim killed with a candlestick in the library, and a real life corpse, especially if the blood is on your hands.

I was staring at my hands when a knocking at the door disturbed the silence. The police? My prints were on the small bottle I gave to Donsaw. It wouldn't take an immense effort to work out what I'd done.

There was nowhere to hide. I wanted out. I wanted those pills for myself, and I'd just fucking gave them away.

More knocking, then Joel's voice. 'Mike, are you in there?' Hours had passed since I'd arrived back. I hadn't moved, couldn't move. The knocking excited Cooper. He danced but didn't bark.

The knocking ceased but it had awoken me. Cooper had been with me the whole time. I hadn't even noticed him. A bark might have helped, but maybe he had barked and I hadn't noticed.

He jumped up, his front paws on my leg. I rubbed his back. He put his nose to mine. I realised I hadn't even fed him today. 'I'm so sorry, boy.'

I fed him. Then we sat and watched the rain. So we did have common interests.

It grew dark. I didn't turn the lights on. My phone rang. I didn't answer or check who the caller was.

Knocking at the door again. 'Mike! Are you in there?' Joel again. 'Your car's been towed.'

There was just no getting rid of him. A stupid fantasy where I murdered him so he'd stop bothering me ran through my mind. I was having trouble working out what I'd do with the body when he said, 'Oh, and the cemetery called. Edward Donsaw's dead.'

It brought home what I'd done. All the hours I'd spent hiding from my thoughts were cancelled out and panic set in. I stood up, paced around. Cooper got excited and finally let out a couple of barks.

'Mike!' the voice at the door persisted.

I opened the door. Joel looked at me and said, 'Jesus, what happened?'

I said nothing, nodding my head compulsively in a kind of greeting as I wondered how the hell I'd begin to answer that question.

'You need a drink. Sit down, I'll fetch something from my place.'

I nodded, leaving the door ajar and walking around the flat some more. Joel reappeared. Cooper danced. Joel talked puppy-talk and attempted to pet him, then he handed me a glass of scotch. I sent it down, felt the burn and the sharp edges within me dull.

'Another one?'

I nodded. He poured.

He looked me in the eye. 'What happened, Mike?'

I hadn't thought about it for a day and night, hadn't thought about what I'd tell anyone if they asked, about what I'd filter.

'I killed him,' I said.

Joel raised an eyebrow. 'Excuse me?'

I finished the drink. He poured another. I said, 'I gave

him a bottle of sleeping pills and recommended he exceed the recommended dosage.'

That got him. He took a step back and stood there for a long moment, taking in what I'd said. He gave me a long look. I'll be receiving that look a lot as I go through the legal process and to prison, I thought. I read disgust and judgement in his eyes, but maybe I was projecting that. He said, 'Mike, let's sit down and talk this out.'

'Take a seat, if you want,' I said.

'Sit down and relax,' Joel said. He could see that wouldn't be happening in the foreseeable future and perched on the arm of the sofa, his eyes on me. 'Why don't you tell me the whole story. It looked like you had an epiphany when you saw that box with no name.'

'Yeah,' I said. It came out like a hoarse whisper.

Joel waited.

I told him the whole thing, everything Donsaw did, up to hiring me and accepting my offer of death. I paced back and forth across my small living room, taking sips of scotch, occasionally pausing to hear the rain.

Joel hung on every word. His expression was very dark by the time I finished. He was looking at me, burning eyes that reminded me of Donsaw's. It was hard to meet his gaze.

We drank in silence. It seemed time stopped having a meaning for anyone after they heard the story of Edward Donsaw.

'One of the sons found him,' Joel said. 'Wasn't long before someone called the cemetery about burial. When I heard, obviously I was curious to find out as much as I could. If what you say is true, they've covered it up. There was no mention of any pills. They're not treating it as suspicious. The way he lived for decades, and the amount of alcohol that was in his system, it hasn't come as a surprise to anyone. The death was pronounced as misadventure.'

That was a twist in the tale I hadn't been expecting. Pills spelt suicide, and that would be messy and unseemly for the Donsaws.

'Why...' he began. He paused, troubled. 'Why a coffin for the child?'

I shook my head and shrugged, envying Joel's stillness, as I paced around like a dog trying to catch its tail.

Joel said, 'Men like Donsaw are very *proper*. I don't think he could resist the ceremony of a proper burial. It could have been his way of dealing with what he'd done, a way to deal with the guilt, a way to honour his innocent victim. Perhaps he *wanted* to be caught one day?'

'Caught by who?' I said. 'Everyone that knew about it were bought off or threatened to silence.'

'*You* caught him,'

'And I gave him his sentence.'

'He sentenced himself.'

I paced. Joel tilted the bottle of scotch without reaching forward, gesturing I'd have to come closer for another drink, sit down even. I resisted.

'What made you think of handing him a bottle of sleeping pills?'

I had to stop and think. 'When I figured he wanted me to hand him a sentence... it's a textbook detective move. Poirot does it in *Murder of Roger Ackroyd*. Detective Matt Scudder does it in *Sins of the Fathers*.'

Joel studied me for a time. 'This is how you make it through,' he said.

'What?'

'When you told me Alison's story; I said, I don't know how you made through. You said, this job, keeping busy. Did you hand all the men responsible for her death a vial of pills?'

He was playing detective. I hated being on the receiving end. It was like a punch in the gut.

Joel looked at the book-wall. 'Being a detective, living out all those stories you read. That means getting the guys who were responsible, right?'

'I've confessed enough to you for an evening.'

'You might feel better if you confessed it all, especially considering I pretty much know everything.'

'What?'

'That night in the Woodman when you wanted to buy everyone a drink and spin them a yarn. You told them about the rockstar and his mother's suicide. And you talked about the piano player getting shot, and how you made them all pay.'

'You didn't tell me I'd said that much.'

'I didn't see any good in telling you. Until now.'

'Oh, god.'

'I've said it before. You have to learn to hold your liquor better to be a real detective.'

I leaned against the wall and looked down at the Archway road, the endless run of traffic. I extended my glass for a refill. He came to pour the drink, then took his seat again.

In for a penny…

'My job finally came in handy,' I said. 'Maybe the Met were right about me, I *was* skilled at what I did. I watched hours of CCTV for days. I tracked Alison's movements leading up to her death and spotted the private dick following her. He was the lead I needed. I got an ID on him. We'll call him Tracy. I paid him a visit with my police truncheon, a balaclava covering my face, and I broke his bones until he told me everything I wanted to know.

'He pleaded innocence, said he thought he was being hired for a normal tracking job. Then he realised who he was dealing with. The man who hired him, we'll call him Coston, threatened him. Tracy said he wanted out. Coston said that wasn't an option — Tracy had said yes to the job, and he would see it through to the end or else. Tracy said he witnessed atrocities he wished he'd never seen. What was our name for the boss again?'

Joel looked at the floor in concentration. I remembered before he did. 'Barry.'

'Yes, Barry,' Joel agreed.

'Barry was the man at the top of the pyramid, but Coston was his man was in charge of making his problem go away. Coston had psychopathic tendencies, killed needlessly, he killed Alison needlessly. He was given an instruction like, 'Do what you need to do. Just make it go away.' Exactly the kind of Carte Blanche direction he lived for.

'Barry didn't want to touch it, didn't want to think about the situation. Hence, he hadn't even met Tracy. I called Barry and pretended to be Tracy. I told him I'd been working with Coston, had been threatened by him and was scared shitless. I told him Coston was holding out on him, planning to get the evidence and use it himself to get the payoff. I said I wanted to put my lot in Barry, and would prove my earnestness by getting the evidence off Paul and giving it too him directly for free. All I wanted was his word I'd be safe from Coston.

'I left messages with people who knew Paul, saying I knew the score, and I could use my contacts to get his money if he handed me the evidence. Shortly after, a contact of his gave me an envelope with the dirt he had on Barry.'

'Barry gave me an address. I couriered copies of some of what was in the envelope to him, and that was enough for him to take out Coston. Then I posted the actual contents to the police, and now Barry's doing life in Whitemoor.'

Eyes bulging, his mouth actually hanging open, Joel was the definition of astounded. 'Nick's little brat, who was too timid to come into my shop, did all that?'

'Extenuating circumstances,' I said.

'That's... the craziest thing I've ever heard. What made you think you could pull it off?'

'I figured I needed a plan, and the brains to improvise. Plus, I didn't much care if I died trying.' I sighed at my graceless platitude. It was the truth, at least. 'Donsaw said to me, *I know what you did for your wife.* I guess he meant, handing out the sentence. When I worked things out, I guessed that was what he wanted from me.'

Joel ruminated, then nodded slowly. 'Right, he knew what he was doing. He looked like a mess, but he was clever enough to dress up and act like a gent when he had to come to your office and hire you.'

'He did scrub up surprisingly well.'

'He got away with what he did, but he didn't ultimately. He couldn't forgive himself. That's where you came in.'

I said nothing. I was feeling the anti-climax of solving another case and dealing out some idea of justice that felt right. And I still couldn't save her. What I did was never enough.

'So, what about the little brother?' Joel asked.

'What?'

'Paul.'

'What about him?'

'What happened to him?'

'Nothing.'

'Nothing?'

I squeezed the glass in my hand, clenched my eyes shut, wanted to scream. I'd not told the story of the Incident to anyone before. I was feeling it all happening so vividly, watching Alison's ghost on the Vido screen, breaking the bones of the man who'd been paid to discover her identity. And calling Harry Flett, fooling him, bargaining with the evidence Paul had on him in exchange for taking out Coston. And giving up Paul's location to sweeten the deal. An image of Paul's pretty-boy face and cocky expression flashed in my mind, the man who dragged Alison down into his world of compulsive gambling and shady characters in a desperate lunge for self-preservation.

I said, 'Detective Tracy told me they had Paul on the phone, told him they knew who he was and he wouldn't get a dime — only his sister's life. They had a gun to her head. Paul said he wouldn't play it that way and hung up. So they killed her. I wonder if he really cared so little about her, or if he saw it as a gamble and couldn't resist.'

The energy went out of me. I collapsed into a chair. That numb feeling that allowed hours to pass by after I handed Donsaw the pills had returned; or something like it.

'I had to do it,' I said to Joel.

He cast his eyes downward.

'Had to,' I said.

Joel didn't make a sound. I refilled my glass, finishing the bottle.

'So what happens now?' I said.

Joel looked up at me, surprised, surprised something was being asked of him. He thought about it and shrugged. 'I guess it's up to you if you want to hire your own Mike

Seferis to work things out and hand you a sentence. But I don't think there's another Mike Seferis out there.' He looked at the book-wall. 'You've had years of training. You weren't joking about your collection.'

He turned his head to the other side of the room. 'And you have a piano.'

'Yep.'

Joel raises his eyebrows for further explanation.

'Alison's.'

'Can you play at all?'

I shook my head.

'Do you mind if I have a go?'

'You play?'

'You don't live with a musician for thirty years and not pick up a thing or two.'

'*I* didn't.'

'You had other hobbies,' he said, pulling a chair over to the piano. He popped open the lid and counted the keys like he was working out the notes. Then he started to play some basic blues in a precise style. He played slow and melancholy, a simple, minimal style that somehow had a moving depth.

'Damn, you're a player,' I said.

'Half a bottle of scotch helps,' he said, and indeed, the drink had amplified his rich, gravelly voice too. 'It plays nicely.' His sentences staggered and intermittent as he played around with different styles. 'I like that old honky-tonk sound. I feel like I'm in a saloon. You keep it for her?'

'Yeah, the bulkiest, most impractical thing to hold on to.'

'I still have Dan's horn. The kinder thing to do would be to give it to a young musician so it can fulfil its purpose again.'

He was loosening up now, tapping a few delicate jazz

chords. 'I miss him,' he said. 'It was a hookup on Hampstead Heath that turned into a romance. We spent the whole weekend in bed, then a lifetime had passed by and we were middle-aged. Then he got a cough, a lifetime of playing in smoky jazz clubs, it was lung cancer. He withered on the sofa for a few months, then a few days in hospital...'

He concentrated on the keys. Some moments were fluid and sublime. He'd hit a run of melodic notes, probably ingrained in his muscle memory, before things slowed down and he'd have to think again.

'When I came here from Stroud Green,' I said, 'I didn't take a thing of hers, except her piano.' I was at that stage of drunkenness where I felt like I was watching somebody else doing the talking. 'I had to get rid of everything that reminded me of her. Her piano was the one thing I couldn't leave behind.'

Joel didn't answer. He was focused on playing. The melody changed into a tune I recognised. His simple style brought out its sweet nostalgic element. Like a lot of jazz music, it was cool, and full of showy, youthful hubris, but warm and intimate and beautiful. I could hardly believe it. It was one of Alison's signature tunes. I'd never known its name. I thought it had long been lost to me.

Your free book is waiting

A lifelong friend of Mike Seferis is accused of murdering his employer. The police are racing to build up as much evidence as they can against him. Mike has one shot to prove his friend didn't fire the shot in Holland Park.

Get a free copy of the novella: *A Shot In Holland Park* here:

www.sjandrewswriter.com

ABOUT THE AUTHOR

S J Andrews writes stories inspired by great cities, classic jazz and blues music, and old noir fiction. He grew up on the cosy crimes of Agatha Christie and the hardboiled mysteries of Raymond Chandler and Lawrence Block. His tastes haven't changed much. The Highgate Murder is the first of a mystery series featuring Mike Seferis, P.I., and is perhaps a blend of those influences. He lives, works and writes in London, where his novels are set.

Thanks for joining Mike and Joel in The Highgate Murder. They will be returning soon in A Scream In Skye.

If you enjoyed the book and have a moment to spare, I would really appreciate a short review. Your help in spreading the word is gratefully appreciated. You can also sign up to be notified about my next book as well as prerelease specials and giveaways at my website www.sjandrewswriter.com.

ACKNOWLEDGMENTS

Thanks to Rob Cochran and Matt Bayliss for developmental direction, and to Mariëlle Smith for the line edit.

Printed in Great Britain
by Amazon